To Maureen.
Read & enjoy

G000151124

About the Author

I married young and travelled the world for over twenty years with my soldier husband. Jobs early in my marriage ranged from cleaning in a hospital for people with mental disabilities, through to secretarial jobs. Then I took four years out to achieve a BSc Hons (2:1) in Information and Communication Technology and Maths, and a Post Graduate Certificate of Education (Primary). I then took up a new career in teaching, culminating in a headship. Retirement now gives me time to write, swim, do tai chi and attend many groups on offer with the University of the Third Age (U3A) and produce a bi-monthly newsletter for over six hundred members.

The Secret Spy

Lynne Pearson

The Secret Spy

Olympia Publishers
London

www.olympiapublishers.com

OLYMPIA PAPERBACK EDITION

Copyright © Lynne Pearson 2018

The right of Lynne Pearson to be identified as author of
this work has been asserted in accordance with sections 77 and 78 of
the Copyright, Designs and Patents Act 1988.

All Rights Reserved

No reproduction, copy or transmission of this publication
may be made without written permission.
No paragraph of this publication may be reproduced,
copied or transmitted save with the written permission of the
publisher, or in accordance with the provisions
of the Copyright Act 1956 (as amended).

Any person who commits any unauthorised act in relation to
this publication may be liable to criminal
prosecution and civil claims for damage.

A CIP catalogue record for this title is
available from the British Library.

ISBN: 978-1-78830-140-4

This is a work of fiction.
Names, characters, places and incidents originate from the writer's
imagination. Any resemblance to actual persons, living or dead, is
purely coincidental.

First Published in 2018

Olympia Publishers
60 Cannon Street
London
EC4N 6NP

Printed in Great Britain

Dedication

To my mum, Terri Rowntree, for her loving care.

Acknowledgments

To my husband, Gordie Pearson, for his support and encouragement and for his sharing of information on some of the more technical issues.

To Jane's Defence Weekly for their informative articles on chemical agents.

Chapter One

What do you imagine a spy to look like? Tall, blonde and very handsome, like Daniel Craig? Or like someone you wouldn't really notice but who's intelligent, has attended the 'appropriate' red-brick universities, and keeps their skills well-hidden so that they can 'blend' into any situation? How about a retired teacher who is, apart from anything else, a wife, mum and nanny to clever and engaging grandchildren? Sounds ridiculous? How little you know about the world in which you live, and the many types of secret spies it contains!

Ali couldn't get her head around retirement at all. She had joined various groups, some of which involved keeping herself fit and healthy: walking, swimming, dancing, golf, shooting and tai chi. She had also joined some groups to keep her brain ticking along: reading groups, and on-line gaming - Minecraft (Survival Mode, of course), Clash of Clans and the like. She liked the online versions, because she could be whoever she liked. Ali hated the photos people put on these, as they were so false. They were either so contrived or so disturbing that she had quickly developed an aversion to them, as they were usually accompanied by a ridiculous name: 'spunkybottom' or 'cleverateverything', to name but a couple she particularly disliked. She just had a blank shadow for her picture, and her game name was Ninja Nanny.

It was while she was playing on Clash of Clans late one evening that she got a ping on her computer to say that she had an email. She usually left them until later when she was playing but, as it was quite late, she wondered who would be trying to contact her at that time of night. It was from someone called Adrian Smythe. The message was, 'Remember me? Belgium 1978?' Ali sat back in her chair. Belgium 1978?

Ali remembered Belgium 1978 very well. Her husband, Dan, had been in the forces, and Ali was a supportive wife. She had been a vibrant member of the Wives' Club of her husband's battalion, and had served as both Treasurer and then Secretary. She loved a challenge! It was in 1978 that representatives from the various Wives' Clubs had been invited to Belgium to hear talks at various establishments there linked to the military. Ali had found it amusing to take her husband on that occasion as her plus one rather than (what was more usual) she being his plus one. She thought back to the trip, how they had enjoyed the time together, and how they had not been overly impressed with Belgium, at that time, although they had visited it many years afterwards, and found it to be quite charming. It's amazing how our perceptions can change.

Adrian Smythe? He had been one of the speakers at Supreme Headquarters Allied Forces Europe (referred to as SHAPE by lots of people, for some reason, not SHAFE). Ali had enjoyed his talk, and had asked quite a few questions, some of which he had declined to answer for security reasons. At the end of his talk, there had been an informal lunch, and he had chatted to her about some of the questions she had asked, elaborating where he could. Dan had been part of those conversations, too, and he said he had really enjoyed the talks and discussions, as he was given access to information to which he would never have had access through normal military channels. Ali hadn't thought about that trip, or Adrian Smythe, for that matter, for a long time. To her, it had just been an enjoyable and enlightening time, which had given her a broader picture of the strategic nature of NATO and the role of SACEUR (Supreme Allied Commander Europe). It was no surprise that she subsequently completed a course with the Open University on 'Nuclear Weapons: Enquiry, Analysis and Debate', which gave her an even better picture of strategic planning and the deployment of weapons.

When they had returned from the Belgium trip, Ali had duly written a piece for Soldier Mag which had been well-received, and which was printed in the next issue. She felt that she had had her fifteen minutes of fame, and had found it quite enjoyable.

Why would Adrian be contacting her now and, more to the point, how had he got her email address? Points to ponder! Ali wondered what Dan would make of it, but as he was out of the country at that moment, shooting wild boar in Slovakia, she was unable to get his viewpoint. Ali didn't feel worried about the contact, just intrigued.

Glancing at the clock, Ali was surprised to find that it was almost midnight. She knew she didn't have anything planned for the next day, so she decided to go on a visit.

Not a real visit, a visit to the Dark Web! Ali was a regular visitor to Onionland -the Tor Dark Web - and she loved perusing the darknet markets, and scanning the hidden wiki with its mirrors and forks. You could find any service in the darknet markets: illegal drugs, weapons, some very nasty illegal porn, counterfeiters, software, varying levels of violence and so much more. Ali was never tempted to use any of the services; she was just fascinated by the fact that they existed and were so easily accessible. She knew that the darknet was policed, and that malware was often sent to users to compromise the various sites, but it was an uphill battle trying to eradicate such services, which could be accessed with relative ease if you had the specific software. Ali just wanted to know what was on the darknet, so she was often on the hidden wiki, as it was the largest directory of content on there. She would often spend time trying to think of ways that the various markets could be closed down, as she recognised how dangerous those markets were. Ali couldn't believe that millions of people went about their everyday lives, totally unaware of the dangers which surrounded them. Not my problem, she thought.

Three o'clock, and there was another ping! Ali checked her email again, and there was another one from Adrian Smythe saying that he was going to ring her at ten a.m. for a chat. A shiver ran down Ali's spine, as she thought of that saying: 'someone walking over your grave...' She gave herself a shake and laughed out loud, thinking that she'd been on the darknet for too long, and that it was making her imagination run riot. Feeling very tired, Ali trotted up to bed and went to sleep almost immediately. Her dream that night was very strange, so, when she woke up at eight a.m., Ali didn't feel refreshed at all. She realised that she had been more disturbed by the two emails than she'd thought. What to do next?

After a few minutes of mulling over the situation while she was in the shower, Ali decided that she would Google Adrian's name, and see what she could find out about him. He must have progressed up the ladder since 1978, she was sure; so, as soon as she was dressed, she flicked the switch on her laptop, and began her search. An hour later and still nothing. She had tried every website she could think of, and was feeling very frustrated. Time for a caffeine fix! Ali had taken two sips of her coffee when her mobile rang, startling her in the process. Automatically, she picked it up and was surprised to hear an unfamiliar voice.

"Hi Ali, it's Adrian Smythe. I know it's not ten o'clock, but I now have to go to a meeting at ten thirty, so decided to try to catch you before that. How are you?"

"Surprised."

"I get that a lot," Adrian replied.

There was a pregnant pause before Adrian continued. "It's really important that I meet with you as soon as possible. I can't say any more on an open line. You can name the place and the time. Have a think about it, and email me the place and time if you decide to meet. I have to dash now, but hope to hear from you later. Bye."

With that the line went dead.

What an odd conversation, Ali thought. She hadn't been able to get a word in. She really wished that Dan had been there to discuss what was going on, but she couldn't get him by phone, because there was no signal, and she couldn't really email the details of what had happened, because it was all rather surreal. Ali decided she would go for a bracing bike ride to clear her mind and would decide what to do when she returned. She changed into her lycra shorts and top, put on her trainers, adjusted her helmet, and went to get her bike out of the garage. Checking the tyres and brakes, all routine safety checks, helped her to become calm, and better able to meet the many challenges of the road. Ali set off at quite a pace, keen to feel the speed of her bike eating up the kilometres. She pushed herself very hard, focussing on speed and safety, whilst enjoying the cool breeze flicking up the ends of her hair, which peeped out of her helmet. It was lunchtime by the time Ali got back from her ride. She had made a decision. She would meet with Adrian. All she now had to decide was where and when.

Chapter Two

Ali sat sipping her cortado in Costa Coffee whilst trying to force herself to relax. Mentally, she was doing repetitions of Qigong breath, to help relieve the tension she was feeling. Should anyone have been looking at her, they would not have been aware of what she was doing, and why. That was the amazing thing about tai chi; it was so simple and so powerful for the body and the mind! The seat which she had chosen faced the entrance, so that she could keep an eye on who came into the coffee shop and who left. She had barely sat down in her seat when Adrian appeared at her side, gave a nod of acknowledgement, then promptly sat down. Ali felt disconcerted that she had not seen him coming, but quickly realised that he must have already been inside when she arrived, but in a less visible seat than hers.

Adrian seemed in no rush to speak, and it was only when Ali began to fidget with the teaspoon at the side of her cup, that Adrian began the dialogue.

"I suppose you're wondering why I contacted you?" he muttered in a low voice.

Before he could continue, Ali began, "I'm more wondering how you were able to contact me than why, at the moment."

"Ah! Yes! I can see how that must have unsettled

you. I'm sorry; I should have thought this through better, but I'm afraid I'm in a bit of a pickle, to say the least, and I didn't have the time to go through proper channels! I need your experience and expertise to help our government out of a jam."

Ali was even more intrigued about the situation in which she now found herself. She was beginning to feel very uncomfortable, and quite out of her depth. It flashed through her mind, very swiftly, that Adrian Smythe could be quite mad, or dangerous, or both, but these thoughts were soon put aside as Ali composed herself.

"What is it you want from me? What experience and expertise?" asked Ali, feeling like someone in one of those prank programmes you see on the TV all the time. You know the type: cheap TV, and actually not very entertaining.

"I can't elaborate at the moment, but, suffice to say, I know that you have the skills needed to help our government; you would also be helping some people who are in a very dangerous situation. I am seeing the PM this afternoon, and I want to put a plan to her, which will include you. It will mainly be undercover work, information-seeking on the Dark Web to identify some people who seem to control the even shadier aspects of life there."

"Why me? What skills? How do you know…?"

"Everything everyone does is monitored in some way. That's not paranoia, that's a fact. We can always track people, especially if they have no reason to try to hide their tracks. I know you go on the Dark Web, but I also know that you never try to buy any of the services on offer. That tells me that your ICT skills are good; you're either looking for something specific, or are just curious about the whole thing; you've got a good cover on there, and you know quite a bit, from things you've done and seen in the past, to be aware of the dangerous things on the Dark Web. Those things could be so useful to us at the moment. However, I really can't say any more until I've spoken with the PM."

"I'm not quite sure what you're saying but, correct me if I'm wrong, you want me to do something for you which relates to what's happening on the Dark Web?"

"Spot on! All I need at the moment is an assurance from you that if a request came from the leader of this country for your help, you would be up for the challenge."

Ali felt numb. What skills could she possibly have that could be used to help the country out of some sort of situation? Her mind was reeling, and she began to wonder if she was going to throw up. She looked around to see whether there was a camera, and whether there was any possibility at all that she was being pranked. Nothing. So, this was real? No, surreal, she thought, and had to stifle a nervous giggle. She stared straight into Adrian's steely grey eyes before speaking again.

"The PM? Me? Helping the country? Anything else?"

Adrian broke into a grin. She'd forgotten what a handsome man he was, and how his eyes twinkled when he was amused. Ali suddenly felt rather uncomfortable, sitting with this handsome man, in, of all places, Costa Coffee, and having this extremely weird conversation. She struggled to focus on what Adrian was saying.

"I know how ridiculous it must sound to you, but it is true. Once I've seen the PM, she may phone you herself to arrange a meeting, but it will all have to be very low key. What we have to do is quite dangerous, but necessary. You will have someone to watch your back and you shouldn't be in any danger, but I can't guarantee that one hundred per cent. I am going to leave you to ponder what I've said, and I will be in touch tomorrow."

Adrian passed her a card with two phone numbers on. No names or addresses, just two numbers on an innocuous-looking white card.

"The first number is only to be used in an emergency. If you need help, or need to speak with me, you phone that one, and when it is answered and you are asked who it is you want to speak to, you just say 'Mr. Green'. You will be told that he's not there, but will get back to you as soon as he is free. If you do this, I will know to contact you immediately, and I will do it to this phone." He handed her a very basic phone. "I will give you instructions later about the second number on the card. Do not, under any circumstances, phone that number. There may be a time in the future when you will need to do so, but that time's not now! I know how crazy this all must sound to you, but I can't say any more at the moment. I have to go. Wait for my call."

Before Ali could say a word, Adrian was gone. She sat there stunned. What the hell was going on? She remained in her seat for a few minutes longer and then left the coffee shop, deep in thought, as she made her way to the car park. What the hell indeed!

Chapter Three

Driving home from her meeting, Ali had to focus on her driving, because the traffic was very heavy. Some drivers seemed to be doing strange things which were obvious signs of non- concentration. Ali decided that she would give her full concentration to her driving, as she was determined not to become another statistic on the roads.

To make matters even worse, a heavy storm had sprung up, and her wipers were struggling to keep her windscreen clear. Ali hadn't realised that she was taking deep breaths to help her keep calm, and not allow herself to become distracted. Some of the tai chi moves they did in the classes she attended were so good that she often did them without really thinking about it. The moves, however, didn't stop the thought popping into her head that the people you really, really needed to advise you were invariably unavailable when you needed them. She knew that if Dan had been at home, she would have had sound counsel on the bizarre situation which seemed to be unfolding.

Arriving home after quite a tortuous journey, Ali changed into her pyjamas, made herself a large steaming cup of jasmine tea, and went into the lounge to put on some soothing music. She wouldn't normally get into pyjamas this early in the day, but she knew that she wouldn't be going out again, and she also knew that she needed to think things through, so anything that would help her to relax was a resource to be utilised.

While the rain continued to beat against her windows, Ali went through the meeting with Adrian. She had thought that he looked well - calm and assured - but as she thought about the meeting, she knew why she had felt so uncomfortable. Despite Adrian's apparent ease and good-humour at the meeting, he was obviously feeling very much under pressure. He was constantly tugging at his sleeve as he spoke, and his eyes were never still, constantly scanning the room. Ali thought that that was probably a good strategy for a spy, but Adrian didn't seem to be comfortable with the whole situation. All the clues were there, when she went back over what he had said. The plot thickens, Ali thought to herself.

After about forty minutes, Ali decided that she would just wait and see how things progressed from the meeting, keeping herself safe, and maintaining a high degree of scepticism. Dan would be home in two weeks, and she might be able to contact him before that, if she was lucky, and she believed she was. Ali took the phone Adrian had given her out of her bag, and examined it closely. She popped into her integral garage, to get the small toolset she kept in there to help when repairing her glasses. Ali carefully removed the back of the phone with one of the tiny screwdrivers, and compared its innards with that of her old phone, which she had just recently replaced. She was not surprised to find a tiny button-like device in the one Adrian had given her. She wondered if the device was a 'bug' or if it was a tracking device. Why should he have given her a phone with either of those things in it? Ali was tempted to go to the police but she realised that the story sounded so improbable that the police wouldn't even take her seriously. They would think she was mad. What a dilemma!

Dark Web – that's where she would find any clues. Ali had always been interested in modern technology, and had developed some software for her own personal use. She had got copies of some of the major products which people had installed on their computers to stop them being hacked. She had a friend who worked for one of the major players, and, through him, she had been able to access the 'back door' of one particular package. Ali was surprised to find that she could do a lot better with the code. Using the basic code, and adding to it, she was able to produce two lots of software, one which she ran just before going on the Dark Web and one which she used to do a sweep once she had logged out of it. The software made it, if not impossible, at least very difficult for others to trace her IP address. That was why she had been so surprised that Adrian knew that she went on the Dark Web. Before she logged on to the Dark Web again, she would scrutinise the code and improve it. She began with a vengeance, and, quite soon, could see that her 'back door' was too easy to access. She was annoyed with herself. It took a couple of hours before she was satisfied that the new software was much more secure. Her log in for the Dark Web was not the same as her gaming name, but she decided to change it again, as added security. Ali decided pi235711 would do.

She loved Maths, so having pi and the first five consecutive prime numbers as her log in would fit the bill, she thought. She leaned back in the chair, stretching her arms and legs, which had become quite stiff, as she had been sitting in one position for so long. A low grumbling noise alerted her to the fact that her stomach was empty. Ali walked into the kitchen and popped a wonton soup into the microwave. A couple of minutes later, and she was enjoying the subtle taste of the simple yet delicious soup. Appetite sated, she decided that it was time to get on the Dark Web again.

Ali ran the first improved software, then logged in and surfed Onionland, trying to get a feel for what was going on through the site. She found the usual: arms to access, drugs to buy, counterfeit money to sell or buy, and the usual pornography in every shape and form. It was a very, very dark place. Ali got a feeling that there were some other dealings going on. She was unable to access some sites, which now needed new additional software, so someone must have put some malware into the system, and the additional software was the response. With its mirrors and forks it could be very difficult to track who had put in the malware and from where. It could mean that some of the Dark Web Marketeers had lost money or, worse, lost the links to their varied merchandise. These were not people on whose bad side you would like to find yourself. Their retribution was always swift, and always painful for someone.

Ali felt that cold shiver down her spine, the one you get when you realise that you're in a dangerous situation. Was Adrian expecting her to put herself in harm's way to help him? Surely, he had his own techie team who could find out what was what on there? What game was he playing? Ali couldn't settle then. She logged out of the site and then checked her emails. Nothing much, except those annoying pop ups that she was always getting. How did he know where she lived? Had he waited until Dan was away to contact her? She began to feel very angry. Without further ado, she phoned the first number she had been given, using the burn phone Adrian had given her. It just rang and rang and rang. What to do next?

After a few minutes, Ali had decided how she would proceed. She ran up the stairs, had the quickest shower ever, put on some casual clothes: dark jeans, turtleneck jumper and boots, then went back downstairs to put on her coat. As she was making her way to the garage, she stopped and glanced around her sitting room. The dark baseball cap she'd bought at a charity shop was sitting by the phone. Scooping it up, she headed out the garage. It took her two hours to get to the large shopping mall where she intended to buy two of her own 'burn phones'. She had stopped at the cashpoint by her home, and withdrawn more than enough cash to buy them. Cash sales meant they would be difficult to trace. She parked well away from the main areas, and in a corner where there were no cameras. Putting on the baseball cap, she pulled it down over her face so that it was difficult to see her features. Her puffa jacket, with collar pulled up, hid the shape of her face. Ali suddenly got a fit of the giggles. What the hell am I doing? I'm now acting like a spy in a low-grade film! The giggles stopped almost as quickly as they had started. Ali recognised how nervous she was about this whole business.

Pull yourself together. She gave an involuntary shudder, straightened up and walked casually towards a side entrance to the mall.

It was very busy inside. Result! Ali thought to herself. She ambled along and purchased two phones, paying cash in each shop. The shop assistants were so busy, and her sales were such relatively small amounts that she was processed with almost undue haste. Ali left the second shop, and made her way back to her car. It was only when she was inside it, putting on her seat belt, that she realised she had been holding her breath. Again, the nervous giggle. She put the car in drive and made good time back to her home. Once she was parked inside her garage she felt she could relax. Within ten minutes she was back in pyjamas and sitting looking at the two new phones. She turned on the first one, plugging in the charger so that she could use it immediately. She dialled 141 (this would mean the recipient of the call would not have the number from which she was calling) followed by the first number on the white card Adrian had given her. It rang a couple of times, and Ali was just going to end the call when a voice answered.

Chapter Four

"Specialised Security Systems, how can we help you?"

Ali, without making a comment, put the phone down.

It was Adrian's voice, and it didn't sound like a computerised message; it was him – in person.

Not for the first time that day, Ali felt totally confused. What the hell was this all about, and, more to the point, what was she going to do next?

For a split second, Ali was totally devoid of any ideas, but then her brain went into overdrive. She could feel her pulse racing, and wondered what was happening with her blood pressure at that precise moment. Was the pain in her chest a heart attack, or was it just a representation of the panic she could feel starting to overwhelm her? She could hear a voice mumbling, and was shocked to find out it was her own. It's at moments like this that things tend to happen, for good or for bad.

Ali jumped as her own phone on the table began to ring, and she was just reaching for it when she saw that the caller ID on it had identified Adrian as the person at the other end. She pulled her hand back and took a few seconds to pull herself together. The phone continued to ring, as Ali leaned forward again and gingerly picked it up.

"Hello, Ali, it's me. Sorry I haven't been in touch but I had things I had to do and people to see before I could get back to you. Can you talk?"

"Yes," she replied.

A pregnant pause before Adrian continued.

"I've met with the PM, and she has briefed me fully on the matter that needs to be resolved.

I just need to meet with you again, so that I can give you the full picture."

"Really?"

"Are you okay, Ali? You sound – different," Adrian remarked, a note of uncertainty creeping into his voice.

"Why shouldn't I be okay?" she drawled. Another pregnant pause.

Ali had to put her hand over her mouth to stop herself from going into a fit of the giggles. She was thinking about some of the 'B' grade films she'd seen when she was younger, and she was beginning to feel like a character in one of those. She knew that the giggles were because she was nervous, and she was trying her best to keep a lid on her feelings.

"If you don't want to be involved, Ali, that's not a problem. Just say, and I won't contact you again. I do understand how peculiar this situation must seem to you, but I will explain it all in due course."

"In due course," was all that Ali really heard. "When will that be?" she found herself asking. "When we meet again," came the swift reply.

Ali knew herself well enough to know that she couldn't refuse; she was intrigued, but she also knew she would do what she had to do to help her country, if she could.

"Okay. When and where?"

"I have an office in London which I use as a base. It's quite close to Victoria Station. Could you meet me in the morning, around eleven a.m. and I promise I will give you the full picture? Now's the time to say if you want to walk away."

He waited for her reply.

"I'll be there. I just need the address."

"I'll text the address to you with the postcode, so that you can Google it for the best route. Make sure you've got this phone with you, as you now have my number in it. I look forward to seeing you tomorrow."

Ali sat back on her sofa, hearing the pinging of an incoming text on her phone. Yes, it was the address. Adrian must have had the text set up ready to send before he rang her. What did that mean, she wondered? The office was in Great Smith Street, quite close to Archbishop's House, where she used to go for lunch sometimes. She knew that area quite well and it was always busy around there, not an isolated location, which would have made her feel, if not vulnerable, at least unsettled. Just have to wait to see what tomorrow brings, Ali was thinking, but, for now, I think I'll make myself a big bowl of pasta, have a large glass of Merlot and get an early night. Not sure I'll get much sleep, though.

While the pasta was cooking, Ali checked train times, and was happy to see that there were a few trains she could catch which would get her to her destination in ample time for the meeting with Adrian. She did have a sudden moment of trepidation: no one would know where she was if anything went wrong. She decided to leave a note for Dan, outlining what had been happening so that if anything went wrong he would at least know the series of events. Hopefully, Dan would never have to read it, as Ali hoped that nothing would go wrong, and she would return home the next day without any problems, but it was better to be safe than sorry. She also texted one of her sons, to tell him she was meeting an old friend from the army days in London the next day, so wouldn't be available if he needed Ali to help with any of his admin. That done, the pasta was now ready, and Ali needed to eat.

After the meal, Ali luxuriated in a very hot bath filled with lots of bubbles, and put a scented candle on the windowsill, giving off an amazing smell of figs, raspberries and strawberries, a delight for the senses. By the time Ali had dried herself, smoothing a light lotion on to her skin, she was feeling very sleepy. She set her alarm and then, slipping into bed in her silk pyjamas, Ali was asleep almost as soon as her head hit the pillow.

Chapter Five

The sun streamed through the window, the collared doves on the roof were cooing in contentment, and Ali slept on, just beginning to struggle out of a very deep sleep. When she opened her eyes, she took a few minutes to orientate herself. She had been having a dream which had seemed very real and quite disturbing. Ali struggled to remember the dream, but it seemed just out of her grasp. She stretched her limbs one by one, like a fighter preparing for a tough match.

Thinking through the day, Ali decided that she would do the note for Dan before she did anything else. The note in question was actually an email. Ali was an avid reader of crime and spy novels, and, in one, she had read about spies contacting each other using the same email address. One spy would write an email with relevant information, put it in the draft folder but never send it. The other spy would go into the same email address, read the information in the draft folder, and then delete it, so that there was no email to trace. Ali had thought this was a very good idea, and she and Dan had tried it out to see if it worked. It did. As a result, they had decided to set up a new email address and do the same. Rather than having to find signals and Wi-Fi when they were away, they could just use the draft function in the new email address. It had become a game which they really enjoyed. The situation with Adrian Smythe could be summarised in a draft email and left for Dan to access when he could. This made Ali feel a lot happier about what she was doing and a lot safer.

After a light breakfast of nutty muesli with seeds and some jasmine tea, Ali had a shower, and chose her clothes with some care. She wanted to be comfortable yet smart, so her black Rocha trousers and linen tunic top, black ankle boots and slightly padded bomber jacket seemed to fit the bill. Her usual makeup was quickly applied, and she was waiting at the door when the taxi she had ordered arrived at 8.45 a.m. This would give her plenty of time to get to the station for the 9.33 a.m. fast train to Victoria Station.

The journey to the station was unremarkable and Ali was soon sitting in a window seat on the train, listening to music on her iPod. Not many people seemed to be travelling, so she had an undisturbed trip, for which she was grateful. Ali wanted to arrive calm and in control when she entered Adrian's office, ready to hear what service she was being asked to do for her country. She must have dozed off, because, the next thing she knew, there was a voice saying that they were approaching Victoria Station, and to be sure to take all their belongings. Ali sat up straight, had a little stretch and began to collect her things together.

Leaving the station, Ali decided that the best route for her would be to walk down Victoria Street, past House of Fraser, right through the tiny market and then down Horseferry Road and on to Great Smith Street where she would find Adrian's office. She set off at a fair pace, avoiding, as best she could, the beggars hovering around Westminster Cathedral. Ali knew that giving them money would not help them, as they were all smelling of alcohol already. The Passage, a charity run by the Cathedral, was close by and would always help them. Ali donated to that charity on a regular basis, so she felt she was already doing her share for them. She did acknowledge them as she passed, saying "Good morning," to which she got the same in reply from some, a scowl from others.

It was 10.40 a.m. when Ali arrived at the building for which she was looking. Stepping forward, she saw the sign for Specialised Security Systems, and was just about to push the intercom when she hesitated. Adrian had not given her the name of the company, just the address. Was he testing her to see if she was the person who'd called before and didn't answer? Taking out the first phone, Ali found Adrian's last call and used that number to call him.

"Come on up, Ali, we're on the third floor and the name on the door is Specialised Security Systems."

"Okay."

The door buzzed open and, as she entered, Ali realised that there was a very small camera on the outside door, taking note of all who rang. She decided she would take the stairs as she was feeling just a mite anxious, and knew the exercise would help her keep herself together. Ali didn't have time to knock; Adrian was standing outside the door of the office, waiting for her.

"Good to see you. How was the journey?"

"Okay."

Adrian ushered Ali into the office, pointed to one of the two comfy leather chairs which were placed near the window, and asked, "Why don't you take a seat there while I get you a drink? Coffee?"

"Okay."

Ali suddenly had the urge to giggle, as she realised that she was sounding like an automaton. She forced herself to sit back in the chair, and before Adrian could ask, she said, "Milk, no sugar, please."

Adrian brought two coffees, gave one to Ali, and then sat down in the other chair, before taking a sip of the coffee he had left. He looked a bit dishevelled, and Ali wondered if he had been in the office all night, and, if he had, why?

"I'll come straight to the point, Ali. The PM is going to facetime you here at 11.15 a.m., so that she can talk to you about the situation we're in. I'm just going to give you some background. Before I do, you need to tell me now if you have decided that you won't or can't help?"

"That's rather difficult, when I don't know what it is you want me to do. I'll just say that if my country needs help and I can do something for it, I will. Is that enough for you?"

Adrian smiled at this.

"That's what I thought you'd say."

A couple of minutes passed, as Adrian seemed to be collecting his thoughts.

"I could go into greater detail, but I don't think it's necessary at this point. Suffice to say that there are things on the Dark Web which are causing us some concern. One of our operatives was working undercover with a gang who sold various, shall we say, commodities on that site. He led us to believe that a catastrophic event connected with these commodities was going to occur in a very short space of time. That was five days ago, and we haven't heard from him since; neither have we been able to contact him. Our worry is that, for some reason, his cover has been blown and that he is now unable to make contact."

"Do you think he's dead?"

It was a few minutes before Adrian replied.

"We hope not, but it is possible."

Ali felt as if a hand of ice had run down her body, leaving her unable to speak or move. Before she could comment, Adrian's phone rang. His tone was flat and lifeless when he answered the call but, from his body language, Ali knew it was someone or something important. He put the phone down and turned to her.

"I need to set up the facetime session, as the PM is ready to talk with you. Please finish your coffee, and I'll be back in a few minutes for you."

"Okay."

While Ali was waiting for Adrian to return, she thought about all of the things she'd seen on the Dark Web and was working out possibilities. Would it be guns or equipment? Bomb- making kits? Ali knew that, between the Dark Web and the internet generally, you could find out how to make a bomb. Was it something like that? She looked up to find Adrian staring at her from the open doorway of the back office. Had he worked out what she was thinking, or was he wondering, like her, what the hell she was doing here?

"It's all set up. Are you ready?"

"Okay." Is that all I can say, Ali thought to herself?

In the back office was a beautiful, old oak desk, on whose leather top sat a large computer screen. Adrian gestured for Ali to take the seat in front of the screen, while he took the one on the right side of the desk. He pressed some keys on the wireless keyboard, and the screen response was immediate. Ali blinked to see the PM sitting at a desk on the screen in front of her.

"Good morning, Alison, it's very good of you to come today."

Before Ali could stop herself, she said,

"Ali, my name's Ali. I really don't answer to Alison."

The PM seemed a bit taken aback, but quickly recovered herself. "I'm sorry, Ali, but I do still think it's good of you to come today." Ali gave a chuckle at this.

"I'm sure you're wondering what on earth is going on and why we've come to you. I will just give you an overview, and Adrian will fill you in with the rest. I hope that's okay?"

Ali nodded.

"We have a situation where an undercover operative has highlighted a situation for us but has then vanished. The Dark Web is very much involved with what's going on. We need someone with your skills to try to find out if what we have been told is true. Once we ascertain that, we can then take the appropriate action. Time is not on our side. The commodities we are talking about are C4, and some very nasty chemical agents. There are more sophisticated ways to set off bombs and distribute chemical agents, but they would not be as easily accessible as the C4 or the various chemicals. An additional problem - and one of the reasons we can't use one of our own operatives - is that the undercover operative may have been radicalised, so the information may, or may not, be true. You're an unknown, so you would not be easily recognised as an agent working for us. I am not going to put you on the spot and ask you to make a decision now. I will leave you in Adrian's very capable hands. He will fill you in on all the details, and give you any help you may need. Thank you again, Ali."

The screen went blank. Adrian sat back in his chair and said nothing, while Ali couldn't drag her gaze away from the blank screen. The information she had received was going around and round in her head and, although scared, she was already beginning to think of ways she could get the information that was needed.

"Okay," she stated, in a calm, but controlled voice, which seemed to belong to someone else.

"Okay?"

"Okay. I'll do it."

"I think what we need to do is go through all the information I have so that you have a fuller picture of the situation. The sooner we start the sooner we finish. You game?"

"Yes." Ali was determined that she was not going to keep saying okay.

Adrian removed the screen from the desk, walked to the filing cabinet, unlocked it with a key and took out an enormous file which he put on the side of the desk. His body language had changed Ali realised; she had not picked up on how tense he had been when she first arrived. Adrian smiled and sat down heavily on the chair.

"Where to start?"

"At the beginning," replied Ali.

Chapter Six

Ali was pacing up and down in Adrian's office, trying to digest all the information she had read in the file. She had been in the office for four hours now, and was feeling quite light-headed and somewhat overwhelmed. Adrian had suggested they have a break - had insisted, in the end - because Ali had been keen to keep going. When she smelt the aroma of the curry that Adrian brought into the office twenty minutes later, hearing her stomach growling in welcome, she knew it was right that they stop and recharge their batteries.

The meal was eaten in silence, as both Adrian and Ali were digesting, not just the food, but the wealth of information they had processed. Ali spoke first.

"How do you know that the sarin has not already been smuggled into the country? In its liquid form, it's harmless until combined with its constituent parts, so it may already have been smuggled in."

Adrian was surprised that Ali knew so much.

"Chatter on the Dark Web seems to indicate otherwise. Although it's not so difficult to smuggle in, it's quite difficult to buy in the first place, and it's very expensive. The fact that someone is trying to buy C4, and not too large quantities of it, seems to suggest that it hasn't been possible to get the sarin. C4, in small quantities, could be enough explosive to distribute a less deadly chemical agent."

"You mean ricin, obviously?" Ali replied.

"Could be."

"Hmm. The bottom line is that you don't really know either way?"

"No, we don't, and that's where you come in. If you can find out what has been bought, where and by whom, we can take it from there. It could be a hoax, just to stir things up, but can we take the risk? I don't think so."

"Neither do I."

"You're our joker in the pack. As we can't be sure about our undercover agent, we need an independent; someone no one knows. That's you. You have a presence on the Dark Web, and are well able to navigate around its many forks and turns, so people making buys, or trying to make buys, wouldn't be worried about you being on the system. Can I suggest that we do another couple of hours raking through the file, and then discuss how we need to move forward?"

Ali didn't have time to think about Adrian's comments, because the door to the office was pushed open with such force that the door nearly came off its hinges. Almost falling in through the door was a policeman, face ashen and eyes wide with panic.

"Sir, a situation that needs your attention, now!"

Adrian jumped up and rushed out of the office, closely followed by Ali. He turned, "Stay here. Keep going through the file, and I'll be back as soon as I can." Adrian then sprinted down the stairs in pursuit.

Ali didn't know what to do. Heart beating, fighting for breath, she picked up her bag, rummaged around in it until she found her inhaler, and inhaled deeply. She then sat down to compose herself. A few minutes later, she was in control once more, and began to do just as she'd been directed by Adrian. A notebook at her side, she split the page in two. One column was notes on things she now knew from the file, while the second column was things she needed to know.

So wrapped up was she in what she was doing that Ali didn't realise how much time had passed. It was only when she heard the door being opened once again, that she looked up from the file, fearful of who might be entering. She breathed a sigh of relief when she saw that it was Adrian. He looked exhausted, as he flopped down in one of the leather chairs.

"What's happened?" Ali asked, not sure she wanted the answer. Adrian ran his hands through his hair and straightened up in the chair.

"There was a problem at the House of Commons. A man and then a woman collapsed quite close to the entrance, within about five minutes of each other. Then another man shouted that there was a strange smell, before he also collapsed. Obviously, we were all thinking that we were already too late to contain the chemical attack. However, as it turned out, we were wrong? It seems that there were some workmen working nearby and they didn't realise they had caused damage to a pipe. There had been a build-up of gas, mixed with the chemicals with which they were working, which caused the smell, and it had overwhelmed the first man, then the woman, and then the second man had a minor heart attack, because he thought he was being gassed."

Ali was speechless. What could you say in such a situation?

"Maybe I should get you a coffee?"

Adrian nodded. While Ali was preparing the coffee, he scanned the notes she had been making in his absence, impressed by her understanding of the situation, and her possible points to action.

"I can see you haven't wasted any time while I was away. Let's use your notes to plan our next move."

Ali handed him a cup of coffee, put the one she had made for herself by her notes, and sat down, ready for the next phase of their partnership.

Taking a few sips of his coffee, Adrian began. He outlined how the agent had gone undercover, after the chatter on the Dark Web had become more worrying that usual. The agent had been located in Birmingham, where it was thought that the request for sarin had originated. For a couple of months, he had been able to make contact and pass on information, but then, quite suddenly, all contact had stopped. Then the chatter had changed to discussions on how relatively easy it was to make ricin from ingredients that could be purchased without too much notice. Distribution of the ricin with a small amount of C4 (too much C4, and the chemical agent could just dissipate into the atmosphere, without harming anyone) was also being discussed. What Adrian was asking Ali was that she go on the Dark Web and try to find out who was trying to buy, where they were located, and whether they had had any success. She would be supported by just one of their techies – their best one – and she would be able to contact him at any time, on the second number which Adrian had originally given her. Ali was not given his name, as that was not deemed to be necessary information. In like vein, he had not been given Ali's name, just the number from which she would call. His instructions were to give her any support and help she requested and then let Adrian know immediately. It seemed a sensible plan.

"What if I contact you on the first number and you don't answer?" Ali asked, remembering the first time she had tried to call Adrian.

"So, it was you who tried to call me before? Not just on the phone I gave you either, is that correct?"

"Maybe."

"I hadn't had time to set that number up when you phoned the first time, because of something else I had been dealing with. The second time you used a different phone so I had to presume that it was actually someone trying to hire my firm. In fact, we do work with security systems for other people, because it's a good cover for what we do for the country. If you phone me now on the phone I gave you, to the number I gave you, you would either get me or someone else who would relay your message to Mr Green (me). Okay?"

"That will have to do, won't it?"

"Are you happy to proceed, Ali? You know what's at stake, and you know why it has to be you," stated Adrian, gazing at her with some trepidation, fearful lest she decide she wouldn't or couldn't help.

"After having read the file, spoken with the PM and talked to you, I have to do it. I wouldn't say I was happy to proceed but I am quite stoic about it."

Adrian gave a sigh that came from the heart.

"I can't tell you how relieved I am to hear you say that. Thank you. You know you can't tell anyone about this, don't you? When Dan returns, you can tell him but no one else."

"Not a problem."

"I'll walk you up to Victoria Station, if you like?" stated Adrian.

"No need. The walk will do me good, help to clear my head. I'll have an early night tonight, as I feel exhausted; then, tomorrow, I'll get on the case."

"If you're sure you don't need an escort, I do have lots to do here before I can go home tonight. Safe journey, and hope to hear from you soon. Remember, we're here to support you, so you're not doing this on your own."

"I realise that. Must dash or I'll be waiting ages for a train. Bye."

Ali traipsed down the stairs, and was soon on her way back to Victoria Station. She stopped at the M & S in the station, bought a cold drink of mango and papaya to drink on the train, rushed on to the platform and was lucky enough to get a window seat. Within five minutes, the train was trundling out of Victoria Station and taking her home. Ali closed her eyes, and was just dropping off to sleep when she sat up, startled. How did Adrian know Dan was away from home?

Chapter Seven

Stretching, to try to loosen the knot of tension that she felt in her neck, Ali felt a bit of a wreck. Had it only been a few days since her initial email from Adrian Smythe? She struggled to digest all the information she had been given the previous day, and, although keen to get started with her task, she knew that she would be unsuccessful if she pushed herself too hard in her present, fragile state. Realising that it was Wednesday, the day of her tai chi class, gave her some hope of getting her mind, if not her body, into a state that could cope with what lay ahead.

After a bowl of nutty muesli and a cup of jasmine tea, followed by a piece of spelt and rye toast, Ali felt decidedly better. She was surprised to find herself humming in the shower, not knowing whether that was a good or a bad thing. Putting on leggings and a loose top, a band holding back her hair and a pair of soft shoes on her feet, she was in the car in record time, and on the way to her class. As she trotted up the stairs (Ali never walked anywhere) she was pleased to see her group of friends waiting to go into the hall.

"Where were you yesterday?" asked Jane, one of her oldest friends. "I rang you at home three times throughout the day as I needed to check on one of the days out we'd booked. I got a bit worried in the end, so I called Alan to see if you were there doing some work for him."

"I was up in London meeting an old friend. We got chatting and lost track of the time," Ali replied.

"Have a good time?"

"It was… okay."

At that moment, Maddy opened the doors to the hall and beckoned them in. Ali loved the tai chi class. They had been doing the Yang Twenty-Four for a few weeks, and they were all beginning to get the flow. Ali had watched some DVDs of Dr Paul Lam, who was an expert on tai chi, and she enjoyed watching him so confidently do the moves which she was trying to perfect. He was not young, but he looked so well, and was so agile, because of his lifelong adherence to the principles and essence of tai chi. Ali felt that it gave her a grounding, so that any issues that came up in her life never seemed as bad as they could have been. She just dealt with things as they came, and got on with life. As they did the warm down, she felt a burst of energy, and knew that, if she took her time, she could do what she had been asked to do by Adrian and the PM. The situation still felt unreal, though.

In Costa, after the class, Ali and her friends enjoyed their various beverages, and chatted away about nothing in particular. They were a friendly group, and good company; in fact, laughter from the group echoed around the shop. It's strange how people laughing and smiling can have such a positive effect on others in the same place. I suppose it's a bit like those laughing policemen at the seaside – you watch them, hear their raucous laughter and you can't stop yourself doing the same. Curious.

Driving home, Ali fought to keep her mind on the road. She kept going over the previous few days, amazed at how much had happened in such a short time. She was also angry with herself, because she realised that she hadn't checked the draft copy in the alternative email account to see if Dan had accessed the 'book' she had left there in her attempt to let him know what had been happening. Looking up, Ali was surprised and a little scared to find that she was on her own drive, and that she had no memory of crossing the various junctions on the route home. Definitely not the safest way to drive. She pressed the switch on her remote in the car, and the garage door slowly opened. Ali drove in, got out of her car and zapped the remote again to close the garage door behind her.

Ali's laptop was on the dining room table, so she fired it up, impatient to get on to her machine. Logging in to the email account, Ali was disappointed to see that Dan had obviously not accessed the account, because there was nothing on there from him. She contemplated deleting what she had written but, in the end, she decided to leave the information there. Should anything happen to her, at least Dan would know some of the background to what had been going on in his absence. The notebook she had used while in Adrian's office was still in Ali's handbag, so she decided that she would read through all her notes while having her lunch. Placing the notebook on the table, she flicked through the pages, while chewing her way through a chicken salad sandwich, not really focusing on the taste of what she was eating, but just knowing that she had to have something, to keep her going.

Half an hour later, Ali was running her software program before going on to the Dark Web. She knew that her task was to find the who, what and where of the people suspected of trying to buy sarin and C4, and, if possible, anyone who had been enquiring about how to make ricin. Proceed carefully, she was thinking. When the initial software had done its job, Ali logged into the Dark Web. Lots of traffic on, but also a feeling of something not being quite right. Ali couldn't access some of the sites. That was unusual. What was going on?

"Technical department. What can I do for you?"

Ali replied, "Struggling to access sites. Has some malware been put on?"

"A few days ago, but you should be able to access everything now."

"Well, I can't. What can you do for me?"

Pregnant pause.

"Well, I could send you some of the additional software we've got in play, but I'm not one hundred per cent sure it will cure the problem."

"It's worth a try. Email me the link please. You do have my email address, don't you?"

"Yep. On its way."

"Thanks."

Ali heard the ping of an email, and had soon copied the link, pasted it into her browser and was running the additional software sent by the techie. Back into the Dark Web Ali went; her searches seemed to be actioned at a much greater speed than before. She could also access all the sites.

"Brilliant," Ali muttered under her breath.

Hours later, Ali was running her second piece of software, as she logged out of the Dark Web. She was exhausted. Listening to all the chatter on there was quite debilitating, particularly as some of it was of the baser sort. You couldn't pick and choose; you had to be systematic about accessing fully all the sites, one by one. Ali had only covered about ten per cent of the sites, and wondered if she'd ever get to the end of them all. She hoped that she would find what she was looking for before she'd accessed them all. She had taken note of some chatter on one of the sites, particularly as a link to another site looked rather dodgy, to say the least: Fighters for Freedom (FfF). Ali would access that from outside the Dark Web, as if she was someone who had happened upon it by chance, as some people did. For now, she needed to take a break.

Luxuriating in the bath, the smell of lavender and gardenia assaulting her nostrils and a glass of cold Pinot Grigio in her right hand, Ali could feel herself beginning to relax. Pushing backwards, she felt the knot of tension in her shoulders begin to loosen, as she slowly breathed in and out, quite deeply. Ten minutes later, Ali opened her eyes, surprised to find herself still in the bath, in water that was tending towards the cool. She eased herself out of the bath and encased herself in the fluffiest towel you could ever have seen. For just a few seconds, she enjoyed the feeling of safety and then, without further ado, she began to vigorously rub herself dry, before she got into her pyjamas. Ali couldn't make her mind up whether to try to do some more searching on the Dark Web, or explore the website she'd identified. Fighters for Freedom won that battle.

She logged on as Ninja Nanny, and dipped in and out of the gaming sites she usually used. She then 'found' the FfF website, and it was one of the most disturbing sites she'd ever seen. It seemed that the site was supporting the freedom for people to do anything at all they wanted to do with anyone or anything. It can't be legal for some of these pictures to be on here, she thought, but then she understood. The pictures were in various stages of darkness, so it wasn't really possible to see what was going on in them; but the suggestion of what was happening would be enough to put most people off accessing the website again. So it could be used as a contact point for nefarious business. Ninja Nanny went over the site very carefully, looking for any anomalies that would provide a route to the real business of this website. There was the same name on a lot of the comments – Muttaqi (Righteous one who fears Allah). Hadn't she seen that name on the Dark Web on quite a few of the sites? Ali felt sure that she had. But what did it mean?

The phone barely had time to ring before it was picked up and answered.

"Hi Adrian, the name of the undercover agent wouldn't have been Muttaqi, would it?"

"Yes. Muttaqi Saladin. How did you know?"

"His name seems to be on a lot of sites, and I've now also found it on the FfF site too in the comments section."

"FfF – what's that?"

"Sorry. Fighters for Freedom website; a really

50

obnoxious space supporting all and any debauchery ... or is it?"

"Not sure I get it."

"The space is so awful that normal people don't access it once they've discovered it by accident. However, it would make an excellent site for personal contacts, messages and the like. Muttaqi's name is all over it, with seemingly innocuous comments, but it could be some sort of code."

"I'll get some of my team on it to see what they can find and will get back to you when I can."

"That will be fine. I've got a couple of ideas about a way we might be able to trace some of the people on the Dark Web, but I need to discuss it with Super Techie first."

"Super Techie?"

"That's just the nickname I've given him. We're working well together, I think, and between us we may have the skills to take it to the next level as far as tracing IP addresses are concerned. That would be a real plus in our search. Something is not right on the Dark Web, and I've just got a gut feeling that we are being deliberately led one way, when the route we need to follow is the other way."

"Never discount gut instinct, or intuition, or whatever else you call it, as it sometimes can be the difference between life and death. Thanks for what you've done so far, and keep up the good work!"

Ali leant back on the sofa and felt quite pleased with what she had already discovered. There was a long way to go to get all the information Adrian needed, but she was definitely more than a foot along the way. A quick word with Super Techie to set things in motion, and then to bed. Tomorrow was another day!

Chapter Eight

While Ali slept, Super Techie, actual name Jo Jacobs, was hard at work. Like Ali, she loved working with coding and software, and it was she who had written, tested, improved and installed software on various phones, to enable her voice to sound male rather than female. There were many occasions when Jo's efforts would be better received if it was thought she was a man. Some members of Arab nations didn't always hold a high opinion of women in the workforce, and would not liaise with women. They were never actually told they weren't working with men, but the voice on the end of the phone sounded male and her name was Jo (which can be male or female, albeit with a different spelling) so why should they think otherwise? Her bosses had no problems with her gender, and felt that they had been very lucky to employ such a skilled technician, who had a real passion for her work. It was a win-win situation, in their eyes.

Jo and Ali had discussed in great detail the feeling of something's not being quite right on the Dark Web (well, more not right than usual!) and Jo was pursuing that lead. So far, she hadn't been able to get to the source of the site they were investigating. It was impossible to trace IP addresses of people on the Dark Web, but that didn't mean that Jo should stop trying. She had, however, had a bit of a result. Some of the same names kept popping up on the Dark Web: Abdul-Azeem Tawfeek, Abdul-Alee Khatib, Nasir al Din Beshara, Saif Turay and Muttaqi Saladin. It was true that anyone could be using the various names, but the first three were known players, and Muttaqi was the name of their undercover agent. Was he trying to get a message to them? Had he been radicalised, and was he working with them? You couldn't tell just from messages. The players could have 'made' Muttaqi, and could be using his name and messages as disinformation.

Taking time to think through the procedures they had put in place for Muttaqi, Jo began to get an uncomfortable feeling. Muttaqi had been located in Birmingham, as they had identified that as the place where the chatter had originally started. What if that was what was intended: if they were being encouraged to suspect Birmingham, while what was happening was actually going on somewhere else? Jo went right back to where she had started the evening before, searching for a clue she thought she'd missed. It took three more hours before she found it. One of the names used by Abdul-Azeem Tawfeek was very active on the Dark Web site. Could Jo link him to anything on the FfF website? If she could, that would lead them in a different direction. He wasn't based in Birmingham, he was based in Leeds. Jo felt her spirits rise, but didn't allow herself to become too excited. This clue could be just another lead that was going nowhere. Go through what you've got slowly and carefully, she was thinking to herself. She began to do that, but couldn't suppress the feeling that this really was something that would help them. Head down, chug on!

Meanwhile, Ali was struggling in her dreams, fighting her way through lines of code she couldn't quite reach. What was strange was that she was imagining herself in her tai chi class, Scooping the Bear in the Moonlight, but instead of moonlight, she was scooping lines of code, but couldn't keep hold of them. She awoke with a start, drenched in sweat and quite breathless. Reaching for her asthma pump, Ali took two long breaths and was soon back in control. She slid out of the bed, still feeling a bit wobbly. A cup of tea and some porridge and she'd soon be okay. Fifteen minutes later, she was sitting at the table in the kitchen feeling much better. She was jotting down what she had to do that day, ordering them so that she didn't get distracted and forget to do anything that she felt was necessary. Her first tasks were to find out more about sarin, investigate how you make ricin, and then go on the FfF website and see what she could find out.

After a quick shower, teeth brushed, hair tied off her face and casually dressed in leggings and a tunic top, Ali was ready to start. Wikipedia was the first stop, and then a couple of other websites. Ali had looked for information about sarin first, and had found many articles about how and when it had been used in the past. What horrified her was the fact that it was twenty-six times deadlier than cyanide, was a highly toxic chemical weapon and could kill if ingested within minutes. Ali felt sick to her stomach. Who the hell could do this to people? What sort of animals were they? She realised, after scrutinising the various articles and websites, that sarin was probably out of the picture. Ricin, however, was a very different matter. Ali was horrified at how easy it was to make, in the kitchen, in anyone's house!

Castor beans, one of the main constituents of ricin, could be bought online quite easily. Instructions given walked you through the various stages of making it, from soaking and cooking the castor beans, through the mashing and filtering, to the adding of solvents which could be bought from many hardware stores. Special equipment wasn't even needed. Coffee filters, mason jars and the various solvents could be bought without raising any concerns. The fact that the tiniest amount could be fatal, inducing nausea, vomiting and then kidney and liver failure, was horrifying. The only light in the tunnel was that, to make the purest ricin, technical training was needed. They would have to look for any biochemist with leanings towards ISIS or Al Qaida. Ali felt sure that Adrian would have that information, or would know how to get it. She decided to give him a ring to update him.

"Hello, how can I help you today?"

"I need to speak with Mr Green, please?"

"He's not here at the moment but I will tell him that you rang."

"Thank you." What more could Ali say?

Next, she thought she'd phone Super Techie. Ali thought he had a great voice, a bit like an actor she liked; but she couldn't remember his name at the moment.

"Hi, how's things?"

Ali mentioned to Super Techie what a shock she'd got when she'd looked up how easy it was to get the ingredients to make ricin, and, even more worrying, how easy it was to make it at home. They chatted for a few minutes about that.

"Sorry, I can't talk for much longer, but I must get back to trying to find out where these IP addresses on the Dark Web are coming from," stated Super Techie. Before she could stop herself, Ali blurted out,

"I might be able to help you."

"How?"

"Well, I know IP addresses are untraceable on the Dark Web, but I think one day you will be able to trace them and I didn't want anyone tracing mine back to me. So …".

"So?"

"I sort of wrote some code."

"What do you mean you wrote some code? For what?"

"Before I go on the Dark Web, I run some software I've written before I log on. Once I've finished on there, I run a different piece of software. This sort of gives me a double whammy. I mean, no one will be able to trace me whatever happens in the future. However, I was thinking that most people just log on and off as normal because they know they can't be traced. If you could back-engineer my software, you might be able to trace some of them."

No response.

"Just a thought."

"Bloody hell, that could just work! I'm not sure how long it'll take, though, and I don't think we've got much time left."

"I know. Shall I forward the code to you so that you

can have a look at it? It may not be a help now, but it may be a help later."

"That would be great."

"I know I'm not allowed to know your name, so I'm going to call you Super Techie, because of the job you do. I must admit, it feels weird, my name not being mentioned, so could you call me Ali when you need to talk with me?"

"I don't see why not, and Super Techie for my name is fine by me."

"Thanks."

"In the meantime, I'm going to run a program I wrote quite a while ago. It was to help me get hold of a product that was very scarce. Perhaps I can adapt it to search for the ingredients of ricin, linked to materials needed, with simple true/false statements linked to and/or. You never know."

"That's very true. Thanks for the info."

"Bye. Be in touch."

Chapter Nine

Ali was scrutinising the code she had written a couple of years before; she was pleased and heartened to realise that she could improve it to search for purchases of the ingredients to make ricin and, she felt sure, link it to the very basic equipment that was also needed. So engrossed was she in what she was doing that she jumped and shrieked, both at the same time, when the phone rang in what had previously been a silent room.

"Hi Ali."

Ali wasn't sure that the line from Adrian's office was secure, so she hesitated. "Are you there?"

"Sorry for the delay in replying. Am I okay to talk?"

"The line's secure, if that's what you mean."

Ali succinctly covered all that she and Super Techie had discovered, what they were now trying to do and what they were hoping to find.

"Great," stated Adrian, without much enthusiasm.

"Sorry if you think I'm not working hard enough, but I didn't ask to be involved," was out of Ali's mouth before she could stop herself.

A loud sigh and then a weary voice replied, "It's not that, Ali. I'm just so tired and I don't seem to be getting anywhere with this. You and Super Techie *are* doing a great job, and making progress, but I'm so worried that it will be too little, too late, if you know what I mean?" Ali replied quickly, "Yes I do know. There may be some people out there who want to make this damn ricin, which is fatal within minutes, and which does not, I know, have an antidote! We don't know whether it's a hoax or misinformation, or whether something is really going to happen. Okay so far?"

However, she didn't stop to let Adrian reply to her outburst before she continued.

"What you need to do is to find out if there are any biochemists with leanings towards ISIS or Al Qaida in Birmingham, who may be acquainted with some or all of the names that keep popping up on the Dark Web and..."

Before she could finish her diatribe, Adrian interrupted. "I'll call you back in a few minutes. I have Super Techie on the other secure line, and it seems she's made a breakthrough."

The line went dead.

"Bugger!"

What to do now? Ali sat for a few minutes waiting for Adrian to call again. She wasn't good at sitting still in normal circumstances, so on this occasion she was like a cat sitting on a hot stove, bobbing up and down all the time. To take her mind off what Super Techie might have discovered, Ali turned back to the software on which she'd been working when Adrian rang. It was obvious to her where she had to make changes, and she had soon got the code organised. Logging on to her protection intro software, as she liked to think of it, Ali then input the code and sent it on its way: its mission, to search and find the relevant information. Now all she could do was wait.

Minutes later, Adrian rang her again.

"Some good news at last! Super Techie has identified one of the names that kept popping up on the Dark Web as belonging to Abdul-Azeem Tawfeek. The breakthrough today is that links with him to the FfF website have been confirmed. Whatever's going on, he's definitely involved."

"And knowing that helps us because…?"

"He's based in Leeds, not Birmingham. We believe the link to Birmingham is misinformation to detract us from what's really happening."

"Which is?"

"We don't know yet but what we do know is that whatever it is, it's coming from Leeds. The chatter on the Dark Web was just that – chatter. However, the FfF website you identified as being dodgy, is just that. Messages are going through the portal of that website at the speed of knots, but in some sort of code. We've got someone working on that as we speak. Things are looking up."

"Okay, so what do you want me to do now?"

"Have you sorted out the code for the search you were planning?"

"I have and it's already doing its job."

"As soon as you get anything back, call me and then call Super Techie. You work so well together that I'm feeling much more optimistic about our getting to the bottom of all this. I now need to go and do the job you gave me earlier."

Ali felt her face colour up, and was glad she was in the room alone.

"Sorry about that. I just got a little, erm, a little…You know."

"I do. No harm done. We're all on the same team."

"Thanks." What else could she say?

As Ali put down the phone, she did feel more hopeful herself, and was pleased, in a way, to be involved in solving such a huge mystery, however small she felt her contribution to be. She checked the program she had sent searching, and then decided to have a quick shower and a bite to eat. She hadn't realised how long it had been since she had eaten, and her stomach was making the weirdest noises.

It was while she was in the shower that Ali realised that she hadn't checked the draft emails she had written, hoping that there would be at least one in reply from Dan. She decided to eat first and then check emails later, as she wasn't sure how much help Dan could be, from such a distance away. She was also getting a bit worried that there had been no contact between them for quite a few days. She gave herself a mental shake; she knew there was no signal where Dan was shooting, so why the worry? He had been away many times before, and she had thought little about it. She giggled as she thought – well that was before I was a spy! Who would have thought it?

Chapter Ten

Adrian was not happy. There was no way he should have allowed Ali to know how much the case was getting him down; it was unprofessional, and so unlike him. He knew he liked Ali, perhaps was a little too interested in her, and she seemed to be able to get him to open up without even trying. Get on with the job, and stop being distracted, he kept telling himself, but you can't help who you like, can you? And that can lead to distractions. He wouldn't allow himself to be distracted again.

Within a few hours, Adrian had contacted most of the people he needed to get involved. Alan Edwards had been his first priority. Alan ran the Leeds office, and he knew Abdul- Azeem Tawfeek as a major player. The mosque Tawfeek used was Zakaria Masjd, in Chapel Street in West Yorkshire. Dewsbury, in Leeds, had a high Muslim population, and was known to have a significant number of families who were actively involved in demonstrations against the government. Many of the families were purely vocal about their views but a few desired actions rather than words. The mosque had been under general surveillance for a few months, because it was known to be delivering a programme of radicalisation to some of the younger men who attended. Alan knew this was going on but couldn't get proof. Security at the mosque was tight, so he couldn't get an operative in but, unfortunately for the mosque, young men do talk. Because of the talk among the young men and their friends, the level of surveillance had recently been increased. Records of those observations showed that the frequency of Tawfeek's attendance had greatly increased over the previous four weeks. He had been seen on many occasions going into the mosque with Said Ishak and not leaving the building until quite a few hours later. They looked to be having very serious conversations by their demeanour and body language, and embraced warmly when parting company. Something was definitely simmering in the pot. Alan was going to put a team on both men to keep track of their movements.

Jan Michaels was the next person to be approached. As a biochemist herself, she knew about ricin, the ease with which it could be made, and the skills needed to purify it to get maximum effect. She had a few avenues to pursue, which she hoped would be fruitful. Time would tell, but Adrian felt they didn't have too much time left. Jan said she would get back to him within thirty-six hours, at the latest. Adrian didn't delay her any longer than he needed to, so that she could get on with her search. Jan was gifted in her profession, with a network of colleagues from all cultures. She would know where to go and who to ask, without making waves. He couldn't ask for more than that.

Adrian had been awake now for almost thirty hours, and he realised that he was exhausted. Deciding that there was little he could do at that precise moment, he decided to go home to get some sleep and a hot meal. He would set his alarm so that he only slept for five hours, then he would go for a quick run, have some food, and be back within seven hours. Good plan, he thought.

Seven hours later, Adrian woke with a start. It took him a few minutes to realise where he was, and that he had been woken by the phone ringing. He jumped out of bed and lunged for the still ringing phone. Unfortunately, he had almost collapsed into bed when he got home and hadn't, as was his usual practice, put his clothes on the bedroom chair and his shoes in the wardrobe, so, when he lunged for the phone, he tripped over his shoes and fell headlong into the edge of the chest of drawers. Momentarily stunned and disorientated, he lay on the floor and took a couple of deep breaths before pushing himself into a sitting position. He looked around the bedroom and caught sight of himself in the mirrored wardrobes. A thin trickle of blood was running down the side of his face and he could already see the beginnings of a black eye. Pushing himself onto his knees, he again took a moment to get his balance; then he was up and reasonably steady. However, the flow of blood running down his face had increased, his head hurt like hell and he suddenly felt nauseous. Sitting down quickly, Adrian took a few minutes to breathe deeply, hoping to stave off the sickness that threatened to overcome him. Within about five minutes, he felt able to move. He stood up slowly, and took a few tentative steps. Not too bad. Looking at himself in the mirror, the reflection was of a man with blood running down his face, a top with an expanding patch of bright red blood and a swollen right eye. What a mess.

The phone rang again, and this time Adrian picked it up.

"Good morning. Think of how good your life would be if you had a funeral plan and your family…".

Adrian slammed the phone down with some force, growling under his breath, and was rewarded with a thumping pain in his head.

"Bugger!"

He walked slowly to the bathroom, and very gingerly washed the blood from his face. In the medicine cabinet, he found a pad of gauze, which he pressed on to the wound on his head, hoping that the pressure would stop the bleeding. He held it there for about five minutes, then slowly eased it off. Blood gushed out again. Damn it, it needed a few stitches. Adrian phoned a taxi, realising that it wasn't sensible to try to drive, and he put on a track suit and trainers while he was waiting for it to take him to the hospital. As it was reasonably early, A & E wasn't too busy. Adrian had phoned ahead, and had spoken with the Medical Administrator of the hospital to explain, without giving too much away, that he was in need of quick attention, as the matter with which he was dealing was of national importance. There was a code word he had to give, to verify what he said, so that he could receive the swift treatment he needed. As a result, he had four stitches in his head, and was out of the hospital in just over forty minutes, heading home in yet another taxi.

When Adrian eventually arrived at work, he got a few second glances, but everyone was so busy that there was no time for the usual banter which he would have expected. He still had quite a headache, but was hoping that the painkillers he'd taken, just before leaving home, would cut in quite soon. Adrian leant forward in his chair, and was just going to phone Jo Jacobs, to see whether she had any more information, when the phone rang. It was Alan Edwards.

"We've been tracking our two friends, and there's been a lot of coming and going from the mosque. There's also been a lot of talk via email."

"What about?"

"Still in some sort of code, but there's definitely something about a journey, as flights were mentioned, and something about roses, which didn't really make sense. A name was also mentioned: Steven, not a name we expected. We think we're close to breaking the code completely, but what is decoded doesn't seem to make sense."

"Keep your man at it, Alan, and hopefully we'll get the break we need."

"Will do, and will get back to you as soon as we get anything concrete."

"Let's hope that's soon."

Adrian put down his phone, and tried to link what they already knew. He went to the white board on the wall in his room, and looked through everything they had. Still some pieces missing in this jigsaw, he thought. He wondered where Jo Jacobs was with her task, and decided to give her a ring.

"Hi Jo, any luck with the IP addresses yet?"

"Not yet, but Ali sent me some great code to help me track them down."

"Ali did?"

"Yes, Ali. She wrote it for herself so that she couldn't be detected when she went on the Dark Web, and I'm trying to backward-engineer it. I may not be able to do it quickly enough to help us now, but I am trying my best. It will be useful for us for the future, just not sure about now. Sorry."

"Hey, I know you're giving it your best shot, but time is not our friend."

"I know."

Neither of them spoke for a few minutes as if both were looking for ways forward.

"Didn't you write a program quite recently that helped to analyse writing which people had done in code, or am I imagining it? I did have a bump on my head recently."

"Bump on your head? How did that happen?"

"Too long a story to go into now. Am I right about the program?"

"Well, yes, I did. It's quite a complex program, but I have had some good success with it. Why do you want to know?"

"Alan Edwards in Leeds has got someone working on coded messages between Tawfeek and Ishak. It just occurred to me that your program could be the break we need. Get on to him immediately, and make the link with the operative he's got working on the messages."

"Will do, Boss."

Adrian put down the phone, feeling more hopeful than

he had done for quite a few days. He knew that they were close to getting the break they needed, but how quickly that would be achieved was the stumbling block. If Adrian had believed that prayer might help, he would have got down on his knees, right there in his office. However, he didn't believe, so his only hope was in the skills and determination of his people. They would come through. They had to.

Chapter Eleven

Abdul-Azeem Tawfeek's voice bounced off the walls in the room at the back of the Zakaria Masjd Mosque. Sitting cross-legged on the floor were nine young men who were totally engrossed in what he was saying, their eyes burning with hatred for the non-believers in this country, and others throughout the world. Said Ishak was one of them. He sat near the back of the room on the right-hand side, so that he could see the speaker and watch the reaction of others in the room with him.

"Now is the time to take action, as the Prophet Muhammad had to do when He had been given the verses of the Koran by the Archangel Gabriel. We must fight the wars against the unbelievers, and punish them for their decadence."

Ishak was not a clever young man, but the life of the Prophet had been drilled into him, and he knew that, although the Prophet had fought wars against unbelievers, he didn't punish them but forgave them, despite the fact they had treated Him badly.

As though Tawfeek had read Ishak's mind, he continued, "The Prophet Muhammad had to fight many wars when he was being persecuted for his beliefs, and many unbelievers were killed. The ones who were left turned to the true religion, and were then spared. We have many wars still to fight and we must take the war to the unbelievers. There are some who pretend to accept our beliefs, and pretend we are welcome in their countries. They are worse than the unbelievers in this country who attack our families, our beliefs and everything for which we stand. You are called to do what needs to be done to take our Holy War to the next stage."

The men in the room were silent. Many were afraid at what might be asked of them in the future; some were eager to take up the cause immediately.

"The Prophet was a good man, but not an educated one. He could not read the prayers the Archangel Gabriel asked him to read. It was the Archangel who taught him the verses about Allah which we recite every day in our prayers and which are now in the Koran. All you need is a good heart and a belief in the Prophet, and you will be successful."

Zarrar Pirani, a young man in the middle of the group, spoke out in, a voice trembling with emotion.

"What do we have to do?"

"For now, you need to do nothing. Attend to your prayers, keep the faith and, when the time is right, you will be called and told what to do."

Pirani breathed a sigh of relief, and bowed his head, so that others couldn't see the relieved expression on his face.

"Let us recite our favourite prayer together, to give us strength for what we have to do."

As they began to chant the verses, only one voice was missing. Ishak was deep in thought about what Tawfeek had said to them. He decided that he had been chosen because, like the Prophet, he wasn't very good at reading and writing. He was good at getting things done, and he felt proud that he had been the one chosen from all those present to do the great thing for the Prophet. He smiled a contented smile, as the others went on with their prayers. He thought about the journey he would be going on in a few days. Ishak had never been out of England and, although nervous, was looking forward to going on a plane. He didn't have a passport, but Tawfeek was dealing with all the travel arrangements, and had said that one would be provided for him.

Their prayers completed, the young men filed silently out of the back room, through the back of the mosque, and out into the street. They said their goodbyes and made their way home, each taking a different route. Ishak had lingered in the room.

"You are well?" asked Tawfeek.

"Yes, but a little worried. I have never left England before, so I don't know what to expect. The thought of being in an airport on my own makes me feel afraid. I don't know how I should act or what I should do when I'm there. I want to do well for you and the Prophet, and I'm afraid I will fail."

Tawfeek stroked his beard as he contemplated what Ishak had said. He realised that the mission could fail if Ishak acted in a way that made others suspicious. What to do?

"You will not fail," Tawfeek confidently replied. "Tonight, I am meeting Nasir al Din Beshara to discuss our plans. In the morning, he will be flying from Leeds and

71

Bradford airport to Heathrow. I will arrange for you to drive him to the airport, help him with his cases, and escort him to the departure area. You will be able to see how he acts, what you will have to do and how you can look confident in that situation, as he is a very experienced traveller."

Ishak wasn't at all sure about that, but at least he would have had some experience and would, he hoped, not be so worried when he had to travel alone. Not a bad plan, really.

"You must go home now, and keep to your usual routine. Tomorrow, you will need to go to the house, where Nasir is staying, to pick him up at five thirty a.m. for his flight. I am not sure whose house he is staying in this time, but I will text you the address after I have met with him tonight."

Tawfeek walked with Ishak to the door of the mosque, where they embraced. Ishak went on his way home while Tawfeek went back into the mosque. Being somewhat of an innocent, Ishak didn't notice the man who followed behind him all the way home. He didn't see the man walk past his house, or walk to a car parked further up the road, where everyone who left the house could be seen.

The man in question, Jim Adams, picked up his phone and sent a one-word message – Home – to the other members of his team. Within twenty minutes, he received a reply – Here – and was then on his way back to their safe house. His replacement, Maura Grainger, arrived in an estate car which she parked lower down the street, but still with the same clear view of Ishak's property. She picked up her newspaper, and appeared to be reading it. You might think that people would be suspicious of a car parked in their street, but you'd be wrong. The car purported to be a medical emergency car. It is common practice for these to park in different areas of the city, so that, if they are needed, they are not all trapped by traffic in the same place. The nearest one to any accident or incident would be the one called to rush to their location. Maura would only be able to stay there until eight p.m., and then she would have to move, as emergency vehicles had to return to the garage at the end of the day. In the meantime, she was able to remain at her post without being disturbed.

Back at the safe house, Jim was typing up his report and emailing it to Alan Edwards, with a copy to Adrian Smythe, to keep them both up to date with what was happening. The third member of the team, Shihab Ozer, was getting ready to replace Maura, who was outside Ishak's house. He would have to be better wrapped up, as he had the graveyard shift, the location of which was up an alley, close to Ishak's. Jim would drop him off and then park close by, so that, if they needed to follow Ishak, they had a car near enough to follow quickly. The system they had worked well, and Shihab, a Muslim himself, was keen to get in position so that the others could move away. If anyone went into the alley where he was secreted, they would just think that he was meeting someone and didn't want to be seen, or had popped into the alley to urinate. It was soon obvious to Shihab, once he was settled in the alley, that he would not have been the first person to use the alley as a toilet!

At about two a.m., Maura changed places with Jim, who was pleased to be able to go back to the safe house to get something to eat and have a shower and, if he was lucky, a few hours of sleep. Jim was reasonably lucky. He had slept for about two hours when he was woken by his phone ringing. It was Shihab and it was five a.m.

"A large Mercedes has just arrived at Ishak's door. The man who was driving it is now knocking at the door. The lights have been on for about half an hour, so the visit must have been expected. Maura is aware. I phoned her once the lights went on, in case I needed wheels. Will get back to you once I know what's happening."

"Okay. Will be at the car within ten minutes. If you have to move before then, let me know."

Chapter Twelve

Ishak was pacing up and down in his living room, worried about the journey to the airport. He knew that the experience would be useful, so he would watch Nasir al Din Beshara's behaviour very closely. He hoped, after the drive to the airport, to have an idea how he should act when he went on his own journey. Alone. Was he going to be able to do the work for the Prophet? He wanted to, but was he able? Ishak then remembered how the Prophet had reacted when he had first met Archangel Gabriel, hiding himself under a blanket because he was so overwhelmed. He smiled to himself, reassured by this memory. Ishak had no intention of hiding himself under a blanket; he would do what he had been chosen to do.

The doorbell rang, and Ishak hurried to open it. He didn't recognise the man waiting there, and wasn't sure what to do. The man gave him the codeword, and Ishak visibly relaxed. He hadn't realised how tense he had been until that moment. He gestured for the man to enter his house, and closed the door behind him. There was no small talk. Tawfeek had texted Ishak the address he needed the previous evening, but had not said what he should do with the man who had delivered the car. Before he could ask that question, the man spoke first.

"I am to go with you in the car. You will drive, and I

will sit beside you. When you take the case into the airport, I will move the car to the car park. Once you have done all you need to do in the airport, you will come back to me in the car park, and I will drive you home. Abdul-Azeem Tawfeek wants you to text him once you get home."

"Okay. It's five fifteen, we need to go."

Ishak put on his coat, and then put his hand out.

"Keys."

Ishak opened the door, and gestured for the man to go out first, which he did. Ishak then closed the door behind him, and double-locked it. He strolled round to the driver's side of the Mercedes, unlocked it and got in. Whilst he was adjusting the seat and the mirrors, the other man got in the passenger's side. Engine on, lights on, and away they went to pick up Beshara, a journey of just ten minutes in the light, early morning traffic.

Beshara was ready when they arrived. He glanced at his watch and made no comment when he saw that it was exactly five thirty a.m. There was no conversation, and no greeting. Beshara got into the back of the car, and settled back in his seat. Within minutes, he was asleep, a quiet snore occasionally breaking the silence in the car. Ishak had no idea that he was being followed by Jim and Maura in the VW Golf which had graced his street the previous day.

"Suspect arriving at the Leeds and Bradford Airport. He has no luggage and seems to be helping the person who was in the back of the car (picture sent to you) with his luggage. Maura will go into the airport, and I will park the

Golf. Will keep in touch."

"Don't lose him," replied Alan Edwards, wondering what Ishak was up to.

Entering the doors of the airport, Beshara pointed to the check-in desk. Ishak walked at his side, pulling the small overnight case behind him. He leant towards Ishak and was telling him why they had to go to check-in and what would happen afterwards. Ishak was listening intently and occasionally nodding his head. After check-in, Beshara moved away and explained to Ishak that, because they had no suitcases, the overnight bag would go with them on the plane. Both he and the bag would be checked at the security posts and, once deemed okay, they would be able to go into the departure lounge. Beshara pointed to a coffee shop, and both he and Ishak moved towards it.

Ishak walked slowly, trying not to spill the very hot coffee in the cardboard cups. He put the flat white in front of Beshara and the latte on the table in front of the first empty seat. Sitting down heavily, his face mirrored his confusion. Beshara put his hand on Ishak's arm and whispered,

"Patience. Breathe and relax. If you are tense or look upset, people will see it and wonder why. You have done nothing wrong. You're just having a coffee with a friend whom you're seeing off. Patience. Breathe."

Ishak sat back and did as he was told. Looking around, he could see people going to different check-in desks; some checking in suitcases which he was told went into the hold of the plane. Some were having coffee like them, some having alcoholic drinks, and some changing money. Beshara explained that, when going abroad, you had to make sure that you had the correct currency. Many of the countries in the EU used euros; other countries had their own currency. If you were going anywhere other than England, you had to change some sterling into the currency of the country you were visiting. Beshara could see that Ishak was struggling to follow his conversation about currencies. He remembered that Tawfeek had said that he was a simple person, without much learning.

"Don't worry, my friend, all this will be done for you. You will not have to worry about changing money, you will be given what you need. You just need to remember that different countries have different types of money. Wherever you have to go, there will be a friend to meet you and help you."

Ishak felt better when he heard this, and visibly relaxed.

"Come, I must go to security now, and move into the departure area. When I'm in there, I have to keep looking at the board with the flight numbers. They tell me when the plane is ready for me to get on, and which gate I have to go to, so that I can get on it.

Tense again, Ishak asked, "What kind of gate? Is it near a garden?"

With more patience than he felt, Beshara replied, "Not near a garden, no. Don't worry about the gates. When you go on your journey, someone will be around to help you. Just think about being calm, not rushing and not looking worried. That's all you have to do."

Ishak nodded his head. Beshara stood up and Ishak

followed him as he walked to the security area. When he got there, he took his place in the queue, and whispered to Ishak to tell him to move back and watch what was to happen. He told Ishak that, once he was through security, Ishak was to return to the car. Ishak nodded and moved back.

Maura had followed the pair around the airport concourse, sitting in the same coffee shop, and trying her best to hear what was being said. She looked in the few shops close by, but was somewhat baffled by the interaction she saw between the two men. Maura could see that Ishak seemed out of his depth and often anxious, but that Beshara was trying to keep him calm and explain. But explain what? She texted Jim that Ishak seemed to be making his way to the car park, and that she would follow him and report back when she saw what was happening next.

As Ishak walked away from the security area, he took out his phone and input a number. As he was talking, he was looking around the concourse, and seemed a bit disorientated. Maura could see how unconfident he was and wondered what the hell was going on. Just at that moment, he closed his phone and walked back out towards the drop off area. Perhaps the other man in the car was going to pick him up there. Damn.

Maura followed behind as quickly as she could, without giving the impression that she was in a hurry. It was a skill all agents were supposed to have but some could just not get it. Luckily, Maura wasn't one of those. Coming out of the departure area, Maura stood still, looking around, as if she was unsure where to go. What she was actually doing was locating Ishak, and making a decision about what she should tell Jim to do. She could see that Ishak was waiting for someone, so she texted Jim to drive up to the departure area and pick her up so that they could follow Ishak when his lift arrived. Jim texted back that Shihab was also in the airport, just on the edge of the departure area on his BMW. Once the Mercedes was identified, Shihab would follow it, and they would take up their other posts: Jim in the car on Ishak's street, and Maura back at the safe house until needed.

A few minutes later, the Mercedes drove past the entry for people departing and stopped right in front of Ishak. He got quickly into the passenger side, and the car moved off, hardly giving him time to close the door. Maura managed unobtrusively to get a picture of the Mercedes' number plate and send it to Shihab. Five minutes later she got the reply for which she was waiting: "On the job."

Maura discussed with Jim the interaction that she'd seen between Beshara and Ishak, and how it had puzzled her. She realised that it was some sort of run through, but for what, she wasn't sure. It just had the feel of a training exercise, but a very simple one. Curious. Maura found it hard to believe that this seemingly innocent young man could be involved in whatever they were worrying might happen. However, it was a sobering thought that innocent people had been used before by the people with whom they were dealing. Jim, as the senior agent, told Maura to make sure she put everything in her report: what she'd seen *and* what she'd felt.

Meanwhile, Shihab followed the Mercedes back to Ishak's. He made sure that he had a few cars between them and his bike, so that it wasn't obvious (he hoped) that they were being followed. There was no interaction between Ishak and the driver of the Mercedes. Ishak got out of it, the man drove off,and Ishak went into his house. Very strange.

Chapter Thirteen

Adrian was sifting through the reports from Alan Edward's Holy Trinity – three of his best operatives who worked so well as a team in any situation. Their reports were factual, but included observations and feelings which, Adrian knew from experience, were often the difference between success and failure when hunting a prey, especially when the reports were from such a dynamic team.

He had spent some time on the paperwork which he had received outlining Said Ishak's life – not much of one really. A persistent underachiever at school, he had struggled with education, and was now in a dead-end job stacking shelves in a supermarket. In Ishak's case, unlike some others, it wasn't just a job to get some money or until they got a better job; this was his job for life. Comparing Ishak's life to Abdul-Azeem Tawfeek's was very interesting. Never the twain shall meet, he would have said, but they had met, and they were definitely, if not friends, at least acquaintances with some sort of purpose. It wouldn't be the first time innocents had been used as 'donkeys' or 'tools' to achieve a purpose. Was this one of them?

His thoughts were interrupted by an email from his office, saying that there had been a call from Ali for Mr Green.

"Hi Ali, what can I do for you?"

"It's more what can I do for you?"

"Okay. What can you do for me?" He felt his face flush as he said this, thinking how twee it sounded. He was glad that he was in his office where no one could see. No distractions, he reminded himself.

"Well, the program I sent searching has come up with some recent purchases of castor beans. Not small amounts, but amounts like twenty-two tons. All within the past few months. It's not illegal to buy them, but it's strange that people who have no reason to be buying them at all are buying vast quantities. In similar areas, quite a few hardware shops have sold – mainly for cash – lots of solvents. Super Techie is trying to link up the addresses. He's also looking at purchase of mason jars, and excessive amounts of coffee filters. I'm obviously not able to access the information at the level he can."

"Well, that's really good news."

"That I can't access the information?"

"No. That you've found the links to the purchases. Great work."

"Oh. Thanks. Sorry, not much sleep in the past twenty-four hours."

"No problem. You didn't say in which area you'd found the links."

"Leeds and Wakefield. Super Techie is tracing the addresses, and looking for known names or family members or friends of known names. He sounded optimistic when I spoke with him."

"That's brilliant news. I'll phone Super Techie next, to

see where we're at. Thanks for all your help, Ali. Give my best to Dan when he gets back."

Before she could say anything, he was gone. There it is again, she thought. Why would she give Adrian's best wishes to Dan? Surely he wouldn't remember him from 1978? Definitely a mystery there. Ali decided to check the draft emails in the shared account, to see whether Dan had read and replied to what she had written. No drafts in the account. What the hell was going on here?

Adrian didn't have time to ring Super Techie at that moment, as the phone rang before he could input her number. It was Jan Michaels.

"Hi Adrian. How's things?"

"Still not great, but things look to be picking up. Anything you've got might help though!"

"All I can really tell you is that a couple of biochemists, with anti-government leanings, were approached secretly. They weren't told what the job would entail, but once the acquisition of castor beans was introduced into the conversation, they both backed right off. Ricin is not something any principled scientist would use, even ones disgruntled with the government. Quite large sums of money as payment were mentioned, but both scientists wouldn't be swayed."

"Do you have the name of the person who approached them?"

"No. It was all rather cloak and dagger. Some link through a website. FfF."

"That ties into what we've been investigating. You believe, then, that these people haven't recruited a scientist?"

"As far as I can tell, no; but there is another issue."

"Another issue?"

"They could perhaps have engaged a talented amateur scientist, or talented student of science, to have a go."

Adrian took a few minutes to digest this information.

"I hope not."

"Me too."

"We're back to time will tell, aren't we?"

"Afraid so."

"Thanks for all your help, Jan. Much appreciated."

"Sorry I couldn't give you complete assurance."

"Me too."

Silence.

"Hi Jo, it's Adrian. Update?"

"I'm still working on the code in the emails. My program is running, and I'm hoping for something soon. I'm using a different program I wrote to access information on the FfF website. When people click in to the website, I am activating the inbuilt camera on their computers. Snapshots taken are being used with face recognition software on our system. We have identified Nasir al Din Beshara as a regular visitor to the site, and I think he may be the link to what's going to happen. He travels around the country a lot, and flying's his favourite mode of transport. We're trying to identify who does his bookings."

"He was followed to Leeds and Bradford airport yesterday and was accompanied to the airport by a person of interest. Can you check who booked that one for him, and whether he's got any more booked?"

"Will do my best."

"You always do. My main concern is that we seem to be moving forward, but there are no joined up links, just pieces of the jigsaw. Do what you have to do, and get back to me when you have any breakthroughs."

"Will do, Boss."

Chapter Fourteen

Just a few streets away from the Zakaria Masjd Mosque, Mustafa Younan, a young man who had been in the mosque with Said Ishak, listening to Abdul-Azeem Tawfeek's booming voice encouraging them to be ready to take up the fight for Allah, was working quietly and carefully in the cellar of his house. His parents were visiting a relative in Bradford, so he had the house to himself, and would not be disturbed. He felt very proud that he had been chosen to do the important job for the Prophet that Tawfeek had given him.

Mustafa leant back in his chair, and looked at the items scattered on the table. He had removed the tops of the two shotgun shells, and put the gunpowder from one into the other, so that it was full. The egg timers which he was going to use for the two bombs were very small, and would be easy to glue on to the small pieces of plywood which rested on the left-hand side of the table. He looked at the other ingredients which were in two separate piles on the right-hand side of the table: a nail, two wires, a single Duracell battery, and a quick match for each bomb. He also had two Nalgene bottles into which each bomb would go with the ricin. The bombs were simple, and would be very effective in spreading the toxic substance, for which there was no antidote. The C4 that had been suggested to distribute the ricin was not going to be used, as, if the amount used was just the tiniest bit too much, the ricin vapour could evaporate and not cause any harm at all. Mustafa was taking his time, and being very careful. He didn't want the bombs to go off prematurely. He had bought a high-quality respirator, and a new Nuclear Biological and Chemical (NBC) suit, from two different shops, paying cash. During a robbery at the university he attended, a sealed cabinet had been stolen from the science lab. Mustafa would carefully insert the ricin into the bottles inside the sealed cabinet. Although it might look like overkill, Mustafa intended to wear the suit and respirator to make sure there was zero chance of inhaling any of the ricin powder. Getting that toxic powder into the bottles would be done very slowly and very carefully. No tragedies here; just success elsewhere when the time was right. Everything had to be ready within the next three days, and Mustafa was pleased that he was well on track to achieve his goal.

***

Adrian Smythe sat stiffly at his desk. He had just had a long and intensive conversation about the constituent parts of ricin and the two different proteins within it: RTB (the B-chain protein) provided an interface so that the RTA (a modified A-chain protein) could enter a cell and destroy it. The conversation had turned to any possible preventive measures.

"Do we have a vaccine which we could use if we

knew where there would be a ricin attack?" Adrian asked.

"There's RTA 1-33/44 -198."

"Is it effective, and, if so, how much do we have?"

"We hope it's effective, but we've been unable to do any tests which have shown conclusive results."

"Why?"

"The problem is that the vaccine is a fragment of the ricin A-chain that has been modified to get rid of the toxic enzymatic property of RTA, increase its stability and maintain its ability to produce a protective immune response. There are sometimes allergic reactions, and some longer lasting side effects. Getting candidates on whom we can test the vaccines is also a problem, as we can't do it to people, and you know how aggressive the animal welfare people are about any testing on animals."

"Porton Down laboratory: anything better from there?" asked Adrian, becoming overwhelmed at the thought of what could happen if the proposed ricin bomb went off. "They've been evaluating several potential vaccines against ricin poisoning, but are not quite there yet, despite spending many years on that project. I am sorry I can't be any more helpful. We do have some vaccine, but not a lot."

"You need to make producing some more of the vaccine your priority. I'll fax the necessary paperwork to authorise you to do so within the next half an hour."

"I'll get a small team together, and we'll be ready to start the process by the time the authorisation comes through."

"Thank you. I don't have to remind you of the urgency of the situation, I know, but if you can impart that sentiment to your team without their going into meltdown,

I would appreciate it."

"I understand."

Putting the phone down, Adrian looked at the copies of papers seized in Afghanistan. Even without understanding the language, he could see that it was data about ricin development, and the crude graph showed that increasing amounts had been made. He scanned through the transcription of the writing. Adrian was wondering what had happened to us all as a race. We continued to seek out more deadly ways to kill or maim each other, and for what? Religion? Country? Wealth? Power? He grimaced as he thought that, whatever the reasons initially, it was always about power in the end. He suddenly felt very old and, unusually for him, quite bereft.

Chapter Fifteen

Abdul-Azeem Tawfeek had received a text from Nasir al Din Beshara, asking him to be ready to Skype.

"What's the problem; I only saw you yesterday?" asked Tawfeek.

"You have to have a different plan. Said is all over the place. He's totally out of his depth in the airport. I told him he wouldn't be alone, and that there would be someone with him to support him."

"Why did you say that? I had told him he'd be alone. That won't be the case, but I didn't want him to know there were others close by, in case he got picked up."

"What's said is said!" Beshara replied angrily. "Different travel arrangements should be made for him, but the route will have to be circuitous. I have spoken with my cousin, who does all my travel plans, and he has suggested that someone drive Said to London, and then he will get trains to where he's going. We've got people in all the places where he'll need to stop, so that he can be guided that way. There's less chance of his being picked up, and security's not so tight either."

Tawfeek stroked his beard, something he did when he needed to think, and, after a couple of minutes, he nodded his head.

"Okay. Get your cousin to get the ball rolling. In five

days, Said will need to be at his destination to plant and detonate the bombs. I will send you the details of his passport via the FfF website. Obviously, the passport won't be in his name. I will say in my email 'and my friend...' So that your cousin will know that that's the name for the tickets. Okay?"

"Yes. My cousin doesn't know there's anything happening; he just knows I've got a friend who needs to get to somewhere by a certain time. He may suspect, but he is loyal, and, as we both know, you don't see what you don't want to see."

Tawfeek laughed at this, "Very true, very true. Thank you, my friend."

When he'd closed the Skype call down, Tawfeek checked his phone, where he found a text from Said saying that he was at home if Tawfeek wanted to speak with him. Tawfeek returned the text with a request asking Said to meet him at the mosque in two hours.

Tawfeek was waiting in the back room of the mosque when Said arrived. They exchanged a greeting, and then both of them sat on the floor. Said was the first to speak.

"I thought I was going to be alone on the plane, but Nasir al Din Beshara said that there would be someone there to support me. Why am I not being told the truth?"

Tawfeek could feel himself getting angry, but he pushed his anger away, put a pained expression on his face, and replied. "You would have been alone. However, we always try to put someone else on the same plane, so that if they see our people getting in trouble or looking worried, they can help. We never tell the people who are on their mission that this is happening. It's just a safety measure for them. We would never lie to you"

"Oh," replied Said, who was struggling to understand what he'd been told.

"You don't have to worry, though, as we've now changed the plan, so you'll be driven up to London in a car and will then be travelling on trains. There'll be a few stops, but you will be met at these and supported on to your destination. In five days, you will be where you should be and ready to plant the two bombs. You, the chosen one of the Prophet, will do this marvellous thing for Him."

Said just glanced at him blankly.

Tawfeek continued. "Everything will be ready in three days, then you will start your journey. Let's now pray together from the Koran, using the words of the Prophet, to give us courage and support us in what we have to do."

The two voices joined in prayer, reciting some of the beautiful words from the Koran: one enjoying the words of the Prophet, and one having a warped understanding of the meaning of the words to suit his purpose.

In the cellar of the house close to the mosque, Mustafa Younan worked on, coming slowly closer to completing his part of the mission.

When he returned home from the mosque, Tawfeek sent the passport details to Beshara's cousin via the FfF website. The name he sent was Muttaqi Saladin, and the passport number was for Saladin's passport. He and Ishak had a vague resemblance, thought Tawfeek, and who ever really looked at passports closely when they were men with long beards wearing traditional clothes? Tawfeek laughed to himself, thinking that Muttaqi didn't need his passport as he was in a deep place – very deep!

What Tawfeek didn't know was that Ali had been on the Dark Web snooping around and had then gone on the FfF website to see what, if anything was happening on there. She was surprised to see a message, in code, but with what was obviously Muttaqi Saladin's name. Ali could see that Tawfeek hadn't realised that the website was being monitored, and he and his associates were getting a bit careless. She decided to phone Super Techie to share the knowledge. However, the phone went to voicemail so she just left a message asking Super Techie to call her when free about the interesting website they'd been perusing. We can use code too, she thought to herself. No news from Dan, no news from Adrian, and unable to contact Super Techie, Ali decided to get her bike out. A good run out would help get her brain cells going, and maybe help to clarify the many points running riot in her brain. It couldn't hurt, and the exercise would do her good.

Chapter Sixteen

Nasir al Din Beshara's cousin, Saif, was checking the trains for Muttaqi Saladin's journey. The fact that Muttaqi would be travelling by car to London made it much easier to plan, as Saif could track back from the final destination and give a time for him to be at St Pancras, in three days' time. The 5.04 p.m. from St Pancras would arrive in Brussels at 8.24 p.m. After a few hours' break, the journey would continue from Brussels South Railway Station at 1.11 a.m. the next day, to arrive in Rostock Stadthofen at 1.05 p.m. There wouldn't be time to get the next train to the final destination, as it departed from Rostock at 1.37 p.m., and thirty-two minutes was not enough time to get to the appropriate platform, especially if the previous train had been delayed for any reason. Muttaqi would just have to spend a night in Rostock, and continue on the next day. That's his problem, thought Saif, wondering why Muttaqi wanted to travel such a roundabout route, when he could just have got on a plane? Not my problem either. Saif sent the information to Tawfeek through the FfF website, and got a reply back within half an hour, telling him to book the seats. Brilliant, he thought, while working out the booking fee.

After authorising the tickets, Tawfeek texted Mustafa Younan on one of his burn phones, asking if the job was on track. Mustafa replied that the job was well on track, and would be finished half a day early. Not long now.

Tawfeek then sent two messages via the FfF website. The first to ensure Said was met in Brussels, and escorted to his connection, and a second message to arrange for him to have overnight accommodation while in Rostock, and then be escorted to catch the train to his final destination. The messages were in code, and were sent without mention of the various locations. Tawfeek thought it great that he didn't have to mention where Said would be met on his journey, and the IP addresses didn't give away their locations either – or so he believed. The actual locations were sent from a different email address, ensuring greater security, Tawfeek thought. Said's vehicle, and the specialist clothing he needed, had also been arranged. All going well.

The people who had received the messages were making sure that they had everything in place to meet their visitor. They had been told that he was a special guest, who had to be well looked after, as he was on a very important mission. The only people who knew the true extent of Said's mission were those who would meet him at his final destination, and arrange for him to have everything he needed to complete the job he had been given. The other people were, in many ways, innocents like Said.

In his house, still not aware of the surveillance on him, Said was getting his few things together for his journey. He had bought, as instructed, a black backpack, without a logo or anything that could help it to be identified. It had, however, to be reversible, and the other side had to be a very bright, distinctive colour, so he had chosen the one that was yellow inside. Said loved that colour as it always reminded him of the sun and of happy days with his family, many of whom were now dead. He looked around his small, cosy living room and wondered, just for a moment, if he would ever see it again once he left on his journey. Then he felt annoyed with himself. He had been chosen to do an important thing for the Prophet, and he should not be thinking about his own needs. Said put his mat on the floor and started his prayers. He knew that they would calm him and put him in the correct frame of mind for his important mission. I am blessed, he told himself, but he was also quite afraid.

Jim Adams, Maura Grainger and Shihab Ozer continued with their interchanging shifts, observing Said's property, and wondering how much longer they could continue before they were 'made'. If another team had to come into play, it would take a day or so for them to get a system of observation going which would work best for them. Shihab, hoped they would be able to continue, as he knew that his team was effective in these sort of situations; they had worked together so often that they could anticipate each other's moves, most of the time. Shihab, in particular, didn't want another incident to add further fuel to the hate for Muslim people, as he knew that most Muslims just wanted to live their lives in peace. It was only the few who corrupted the meaning of the Koran to support their evil actions. He hoped that his team could stop anything bad happening, and capture the people who were encouraging the young to commit some of the atrocities that seemed to be on the news with such frequency. Whatever happened in the future, Shihab would know that they had done everything in their power to stop anything bad happening. He hoped that that was enough.

***

Ali was taking off her helmet and trying to fluff up her hair, which had been flattened by the helmet, making her look as if she had a square head, when she heard her phone ringing. Rushing to answer it, she almost went headlong over her backpack, which she'd put down in front of her when she got off her bike. She grabbed the phone, knowing that she would either have just missed who was calling, or just got to the phone before it went to voicemail. "Hi, Ali, sorry I couldn't get to the phone before but I'd silenced all my devices to concentrate on the code I'm trying to break. I've got a basic grasp, but I just need to do a bit more to get the full code. Enough of that, what can I do for you?"

"Well, I think it might be more what I can do for you?" Ali replied, suddenly feeling embarrassed that it sounded like she was flirting with Super Techie. "I mean, I've got some good news for you, I think."

"Okay, great, I could do with some good news."

"I was on the Dark Web a few hours ago, and then went on to the FfF website. I found some messages being sent with Muttaqi Saladin's name in them. Not sure what it means but, hopefully, you'll be able to decrypt the

98

messages. That means he's alive, doesn't it?"

A pregnant pause.

"It may do, but they could be talking about disposing of his body."

"Oh! I thought… I thought…" stammered Ali.

"I know. It's best not to think about it. Nothing we can do either way. Let's keep hopeful, and I'll get onto the FfF website and see what I can do. Thanks, Ali."

"That's okay. Wish I could have done more."

The phone rang again immediately.

"Did you forget to tell me something?" asked Ali.

"Not that I can think of," replied Adrian.

Another pregnant pause while Ali gathered her wits about her, after realising it wasn't Super Techie.

"Oh Adrian, you must think I'm a right twit?"

"No, I don't, but I'm wracking my brain to think what I should have told you and coming up with nothing."

Ali couldn't help but laugh at what seemed to be turning into a goon-type conversation. "I was talking with Super Techie because I went on the Dark Web, then the FfF website and saw some more coded messages from Tawfeek, which included Muttaqi Saladin's name. He's going to go on there now, to see if he can decode them, or enough of them to give us some more useful information."

"That's good news. The message traffic is much heavier so whatever they're hoping is going to happen must be getting close. If Super Techie can decode the messages, we may get a strong lead."

"We live in hope," replied Ali. "Indeed we do."

"Let me know if there's anything else you need me to

do. I must ring off, as I've just come in from a bike ride and I really need to get out of my soggy clothes and into the shower."

"No problem. Will keep in touch," Adrian responded, a slight quiver in his voice.

Adrian was glad Ali wasn't there to see his heightened colour. Why should thinking about Ali in the shower make him so distracted? He wasn't a teenage boy, was he?

Chapter Seventeen

Abdul-Azeem Tawfeek's voice echoed through the room, as the young men in front of him looked on in awe. Tawfeek had a rich baritone voice, which, when impassioned by the hate he felt, was almost hypnotic. This was one of those days.

"Pray for the courage of the Prophet, so that you can take our beliefs forward, and strike down those who lead such void and empty lives. Pray the Koran, and open your hearts..."

After half an hour, Tawfeek felt the attention of the young men slipping, so he fell silent for a couple of minutes, and then led them in prayer. He knew by heart the beautiful prayers, but he also knew how to twist their meaning, to make sure the young men were ready to do whatever work he told them. He was very happy today, as Mustafa Younan was here, and the bombs were ready. Tawfeek could see that Mustafa was very pleased with himself by the way he sat, back straight and eyes shining; Tawfeek realised that he would have to emphasise to Mustafa the importance of secrecy.

The men filed out one by one, until only Mustafa was left. Tawfeek closed the door, and waited for Mustafa to speak.

"Everything is as you asked. As I had all the right

equipment, and time to do the job correctly, it was relatively easy."

Mustafa handed Tawfeek the small black backpack with the yellow interior, within which rested the two Nalgene bottles.

"Thank you, Mustafa, the Prophet must be rejoicing at your work."

At this, a smile split Mustafa's face, as he realised what a great job he had done for the Prophet.

"However," continued Tawfeek, "you must tell no one what you've done. I know it will be difficult for you to keep the secret, but you must. Everything depends on that."

Although he understood the importance of secrecy, what good is doing a marvellous thing if no one knows, Mustafa was thinking. This must have shown in his face.

"Mustafa, I mean it. You must tell no one!" Tawfeek's voice now had an angry edge and his eyes, too, looked angry.

Mustafa was afraid. For a few moments, he was unable to tear his gaze away from those red, angry eyes which seemed to bore right into his very being.

"I... I... I do understand. I will say nothing. I promise."

As if someone had flicked a switch, back came Tawfeek's smile and he put a hand gently on Mustafa's shoulder. Mustafa wondered why he had been afraid before, and began to think that he must be tired after spending so much time making the bombs. Yes, that's it he thought, but he wasn't completely convinced.

"I believe you, Mustafa, and I know the Prophet is looking down on you with love and gratitude," replied Tawfeek, his voice calm and barely above a whisper. "Go and enjoy the rest of the day. I have things I must do."

Mustafa nodded an assent, and left the room, feeling a wave of relief as he then left the mosque.

Tawfeek stroked his beard, a worried expression on his face.

"Something might have to be done about him," he muttered under his breath.

Before he had time to think more about Mustafa, the door opened, and Tawfeek was delighted to see the person for whom he had been waiting. Abdul-Alee Khatib entered and greeted Tawfeek warmly.

"My brother, do you have what I need?" asked Khatib, the excitement in his voice obvious.

"Indeed I do, brother. How will you get it to the correct destination in the time we have left?" replied Tawfeek.

"You don't need to know that. If one of us knows everything, it leads to a weak chain. I will just say I have friends who move freely and quickly. They are ready to do the work of the Prophet."

"I meant no offense," was Tawfeek's hasty reply.

"I know. The time is coming when the Prophet will be so happy, and we'll have shown the world that we are the true religion, and the world is ours to do with as we will."

Tawfeek took the backpack, and gave it gingerly to Khatib, who put it gently into a small suitcase. They embraced, and then Khatib was gone. Tawfeek was left to ponder what was to come. He was feeling very happy with himself.

Said Ishak had seen the man leaving the mosque, and he knew that Tawfeek would now be waiting for him. He stood up slowly, made his way to the room at the back of the mosque and took a moment to gather his thoughts, before entering.

"Ah, Said, Chosen One of the Prophet. Enter and pray with me."

Said dropped heavily to his knees, bowed and began to pray the Koran with Tawfeek. The words were beautiful, and seemed to be calling to him. Enraptured, he gave himself completely to prayer, as a feeling of calm enveloped him and gave him courage. When they had finishing praying, Tawfeek stood and walked to the small window.

"Out there is your destiny, Chosen One of the Prophet. Are you ready?"

Still feeling the courage of the prayers, Said answered, "I am."

Tawfeek embraced him, and then signalled for him to sit in one of the chairs. Silence.

After about five minutes, Tawfeek ran through the mission with Said, making it as simple as he could. He explained why Said was travelling a circuitous route, gave him the names (not their real names of course) of the people who would meet him at the various locations, and told him that he would have an overnight stay with 'friends' before going on to his final destination. All the equipment and clothes needed would be ready and waiting too. All Said had to do was to set the timers, plant the bombs at the required time, and get as far away as possible. What Tawfeek didn't tell Said was that he probably wouldn't get far enough away to avoid the ricin, or that the chance of his surviving the bomb blast, with its toxic contents, was virtually nil. An acceptable casualty of war, thought Tawfeek. Said didn't have any questions. He knew that he was being picked up by car to be taken to London to get the first train, then he would be met at the various locations, and people at his final destination would have all he would need. Tawfeek walked him to the door of the mosque, embraced him, and then went back inside. Said began the short walk back to his house, still unaware of his shadow, Shihab Ozer.

Once Said was back in his house, there was a shift change. Maura Grainger sat in a car a few streets away, while Jim Adams moved unobtrusively into the alleyway. Shihab began his report as soon as he got to the safe house, and sent it immediately to his boss Alan Edwards, with a copy to Adrian Smythe. He described in detail the man whom he had seen enter and leave the mosque, and what a warm embrace Tawfeek had given to Ishak. He also included his own 'gut feeling' that he felt that whatever was going to happen, was going to happen soon. There was just something in Tawfeek's and Said's body language that supported that: one in control and one being controlled. But to what end, Shihab wondered?

Chapter Eighteen

Jo Jacobs ran her hands through her short, spiky hair, and sighed. She couldn't remember the last time she'd had any sleep. She'd snatched the odd half an hour where she could, but nothing of any duration. Jo knew she was on the verge of exhaustion, so she had a decision to make: plough on regardless, or shut everything down, so that she could get a consistent amount of sleep. No contest. To be more productive, Jo would have to sleep, as she knew that she was achieving less and less as time went on. By the time she'd switched off phones, muted the sound on her bank of computers, and turned off the printers, she was on her last legs. Jo plopped down on to the sleeping bag, tapped her head four times, and fell into a deep sleep. If all went as she hoped, she would have four hours sleep, and then be ready to continue her work.

In her dreams, Jo could see lines of code flying around, evading capture at every turn. She, herself, was flying behind the code, reaching out and almost catching the most elusive pieces. Roses were flying underneath her, pricking her skin with their thorns if they came too close. Jo jumped in her sleep, and then, suddenly, she was completely awake.

"It can't have been four hours," she muttered to herself. But it was. Jo had slept the sleep of the dead for four hours, and now, awake, she was ready to tackle the code.

Her first task was to check the programs which were searching for the names and addresses of people who had bought any of the items needed to make ricin. Jo felt it was significant that hardware shops in Leeds and Wakefield had shown an increase in the sale of solvents over the past three weeks. Hardware departments in some of the bigger DIY stores had similar results in the same areas. All had been bought with cash, but the sale of a large amount of coffee filters from a shop close to one of the larger DIY stores had pointed to an IP address of someone living close to the Zakaria Masjd Mosque. Jo didn't believe in coincidences, so she passed this information on to Alan Edwards, to see whether his team could scope out the address which purported to be relevant to the IP address previously identified. She felt, rather than knew, that this was a significant find.

On receiving the address from their boss, Shihab Ozer did a walk past the address he'd been given. Jim Adams was in the alley opposite Said's house, and Maura Grainger was in the car a few streets away, waiting to give assistance wherever it was needed. Shihab hadn't gone much past the address he'd been given when the door opened, and a man came out and headed for a car on the other side of the road. Shihab recognised him immediately as the man who had driven the car to Said's house, accompanying him to the airport. Without increasing his pace, Shihab took out his phone, and called Maura. He gave her the make, colour and registration of the car, and the direction in which it was now headed, while he made his way back to the safe house to contact Alan Edwards. Shihab had alerted Jim, in case the man was again on his way to Said's. Getting closer, he thought.

Jo was now back on the code, working with one of Alan Edward's techies. They were observing the messages going back and forth with increasing frequency on the FfF website. Both techies knew that they were running out of time; they needed the code cracked now. "What about if we...?"

"No, perhaps we should...?"

They were challenging each other, in an attempt to find the last piece which would help them to decode all the messages. It was slow, laborious work, checking, then cross-checking; and, finally, there it was. And it was so simple.

If there had been an Olympic event for synchronised sighing, the two techies would have been awarded the gold medal. Staring at one another, they took a moment before they spoke.

"So, now we need to scrutinise the messages from the beginning, to ensure we don't miss anything. You start on the earlier messages on the FfF website, while I call Adrian and bring him up to speed," stated Jo.

"Gotcha!"

Adrian wearily picked up the phone on the second ring.

"Hi Jo, what you got?"

His body language changed. Adrian sat back in his seat, eyes shining, attentive to every word being said.

"That's great. I'll be right over. Yes… Definitely… Go through all messages, so we can see how this thing is unfolding. Be there in ten minutes."

Picking up the papers from his desk, and putting them in his briefcase, then grabbing his phone, Adrian moved quickly out of his office and into the lift. He would walk to the lab, as it would be much quicker at this time of day than trying to drive, or getting a taxi. His heart was thumping in his chest, in time to the thumping of his headache. He drank greedily from a bottle of water which he had taken out of his briefcase, recognising that he was on the verge of dehydration.

Twelve minutes later, Adrian was entering the lab, more hydrated and ready to look at what they now had, feeling more optimistic. Jo looked up as he entered, but she didn't smile. It must be bad.

"There's obviously travel involved, as there's lots of messages to Tawfeek about his friend, Muttaqi Saladin's trip. No destination, though, so we have to keep looking to see if they're in other messages. Talk of young men, the Prophet and his work, taking the fight to them – I presume that's us," reported Jo.

"Probably is us, but you can never be sure with fanatics. Get through the messages as quickly as you can, as I've a feeling that it's all going to kick off soon."

At that exact moment, a car arrived at Said's house, and the man Shihab had seen earlier got out of it. He knocked at the door, and then got back into the car. Jim Adams phoned Maura, to make sure that she was close enough to pick him up if Said came out and got into the car. A few minutes later, 'Said left the house', locking the door behind him, and then testing the lock, to make sure it was secure. He had a small black backpack with him, and nothing else. He opened the back door, and got into the car. It set off at a steady pace. "Maybe he doesn't think he's coming back," whispered Jim to himself, an icy finger of fear running down his spine.

Maura pulled up at the edge of the alley, and Jim got in. When Maura set off, Jim phoned Shihab. He told him the direction in which the car was going, and Shihab said he would follow on his motorbike, once he'd let Alan Edwards know what was happening. Ten minutes later, Shihab was on the motorbike and trying to make up the distance the car had already covered. It wasn't long before he was playing leapfrog with Maura, so that the driver of Said's car wasn't aware he was being followed. The plot thickened.

In the back of the car, Said sat with his eyes closed, trying his best to breathe and not panic. He prayed that he would have the courage of the Prophet to do what had to be done. He thought about what Tawfeek had said to him, and how they had prayed together. It will all be okay, he consoled himself, because I am the Chosen One of the Prophet.

Chapter Nineteen

"Hi, Adrian. Looks like Said's on the move. He was picked up by car, and is currently on the M1 heading South. My team are tailing him."

"Hi, Alan, how do you know he's not just going to visit someone?"

"Looked like a final farewell when he left Tawfeek at the mosque, just something in their body language, the team thought. Then he's picked up by the same man, in the same car, as the one he used to drive Nasir al Din Beshara to the airport. Said was observed leaving his house, and, again, the body language was of someone doing a double check on safety, as if he was going somewhere for a while."

"Okay, Alan, I didn't disbelieve you, but we seemed to be almost there with the code and my head's still worrying that we've missed something. Great work with your team. You have Jo Jacobs's number already, so can the team make sure she knows where they are, as it may help with the coded messages?"

"Okay. I'll keep you in the loop too."

"Thanks."

Adrian was straight on the phone to Jo, explaining where they were with surveillance, and how Alan's team were going to keep in touch with her.

"I also need you to heighten the alert at the airports, Jo, as we don't want Said to slip through the net."

"That's not a problem. I have software that can take the alerts up a notch, without much input from me."

"Sounds good. Where are we with the code?"

"I've been working with James, and we believe we're on the cusp of finding..."

"Jo, are you still there? Jo?"

"Sorry, Boss, it looks like James has just found the final link. I'll call you back in a few minutes."

The phone went dead before Adrian had time to reply.

Ten minutes later, the phone rang again. Adrian snatched it up.

"Hi Adrian, it's Ali."

"Hi Ali, I'm sorry, but I can't stay on the line, as I'm waiting for an important call. Will get back to you as soon as I can."

"I just..."

The phone went dead.

"Bugger!"

Shihab Ozer was getting very stiff. Riding a motorbike on an open road was great; riding one on the M1 was torture. Apart from the fact he had to keep to a lower speed, as he was tailing Said's car, he also had to watch out for the drivers who seemed to be totally unaware that he was there. He'd already had a couple of near misses, caused by inattentive drivers, and now, even worse, he would have to pull off at the services, as he needed to use the facilities. As he stopped in the car park, he phoned Jim and Maura just to let them know he wasn't there. He then raced to the toilets. Minutes later he was back on the bike, and making up the distance.

At the next services, Said's car pulled off, and both men left the car to use the facilities. They didn't stop to eat, or to have a drink, but returned swiftly to the car and resumed their journey. Shihab followed them, with Jim and Maura a few cars behind. Members of the team were wondering which airport Said would use, Heathrow or Gatwick? As they didn't know his destination, it was anyone's guess.

The car sailed past exit 14 on the M1, which was the turn off they would have used if they had been going to Heathrow. Shihab pulled off at the next services and made a call.

"Not Heathrow, as they've sailed past exit 14. Will keep in touch."

Adrian's phone finally rang.

"Hi, Boss. I think you need to facetime me so that I can better explain what we've found."

"Okay."

Adrian was shocked at the pale, gaunt face that stared out of the screen at him.

"You okay, Jo?"

"No, but no time for that now. We've broken the code."

"That's great news," Adrian began, but stopped when he saw the expression on Jo's face.

"Remember we thought we'd decoded a bit before?"

"Yes. Stephen, and something to do with roses, wasn't it?" "That's what we thought, but we were only half right."

"I don't understand."

"It's not Stephen, it's Stefan; it's not roses, it's Rosenbad."

The silence that followed weighed so heavily on Adrian's chest that he struggled to breathe. "You mean Stefan Löfven, the Prime Minister of Sweden, and Rosenbad in central Stockholm?"

"Yes. The messages make sense now. A country that welcomed them at first, and is now blaming them for everything bad that happens, was a key discussion point in the messages. I know that's not what the Swedish government is saying, but I also know that's what's being spouted by the militants in Sweden."

"Why now?"

"Once we'd decoded the messages, James and I did a search to see what's happening at the moment in Sweden."

"And?"

"Stefan Löfven is meeting with the twenty-five members of his cabinet in five days, to discuss, as well as the usual business, celebrations he wants to take place in 2021, to mark the forty years that Rosenbad has been the seat of government. He's asked that there be some mini-celebrations on the same day, to give the people a taste of what's to come."

"Brilliant work. I need to get in touch with the PM, and see how she wants to play this. Any chance you can get some sleep now?"

"No, still need to keep tabs on Alan's team following Said. We've heard he's passed the turnoff for Heathrow, so he must be headed for Gatwick. I'll get on to the head of security there, and update him on as much as I can. We believe he's using Muttaqi Saladin's passport, and, as far as we know, they have no idea we've accessed the code and now decoded it. However, we still can't be sure of that, so they could be playing us."

"Okay, Jo. Snatch some rest if you can, and keep in touch with me if there are any other developments?"

"Will do."

Adrian's next move was to contact the PM. Using the phone, he had been given in case he needed immediate access, Adrian waited expectantly for it to be picked up. The PM listened in silence, while Adrian brought her up to speed. Although he couldn't see her, Adrian knew that she would be jotting down notes and questions on the pad which she always had in front of her. "Do we know for sure that Said has the bomb with him?"

"We can't be sure. Their usual *modus operandi* is to make the bomb, then get someone else to get it to the place where it will eventually be detonated. They wouldn't want it to go off beforehand, or in the wrong place. The person placing the bomb usually goes under separate cover. Despite what's written in the press, there aren't hundreds of young people willing to be blown up for Allah."

"We only need one."

"I know."

"We're sure Rosenbad in Sweden is the target?"

"As much as we can be. The technicians who broke the code are two of the best, and have never been wrong before."

"Always a first time."

"I agree, but this isn't one of those times. They have been methodical and focussed. I trust their results."

In the brief interlude that followed, both Adrian and the PM were considering how to move forward.

"Okay. I will contact Stefan directly and tell him what we know, and what we're doing about it. Anything else we haven't discussed that he may ask?"

"I would imagine he wants to know whether there's a vaccine against ricin, and that could be a problem, as we have a limited amount. There have been some side effects but it may be that it would be in his best interests to vaccinate his cabinet. We don't have enough for the whole of his population, or even for all of Stockholm, but we would have enough for that."

"I see."

Before she could comment further, Adrian continued.

"The other problem is that we don't know whether Rosenbad is the only target; it's the only one we've identified. The amount of castor beans that has been bought is far in excess of what's needed for a few bombs in one place. However, it could be that they have stockpiled the ingredients for ricin, so that, if the attack on Rosenbad is successful, they have the possibility of making more bombs for a later time and place. We need to keep some vaccine, in case the plan is to put some bombs here in the UK."

Another brief interlude before the PM replied.

"Okay. A very bad situation, I can see, but at least we have the opportunity to stop this disaster happening."

"Agreed. When I had all the facts about the ricin involvement, I instructed the scientists to make it their first priority to ensure we had a lot more of the vaccine. They are keeping me updated on a daily basis."

"That's one piece of better news. Okay, Adrian, I'll get back to you once I have spoken with Stefan. If there are any further developments, let me know immediately."

"Will do."

Chapter Twenty

On the M1, the team were expecting the car in which Said was travelling to leave at exit 6, thinking that they were taking a more circuitous route to get to the M25, then the M23 and, eventually, to Gatwick Airport. They were surprised when it continued on up the M1. "Where the hell's he going?" asked Jim Edwards, voicing aloud his thoughts.

Shihab, just behind them on his bike, was thinking the same thing. He decided, against his better judgement, to pull on to the hard shoulder and let his boss, Alan Edwards, know straight away.

"Stick close to the bike, Shihab. If he's going into Central London, Maura and Jim may lose him in the car. He may be going to London Airport. Put your GPS program on, and we'll track you with that, so that you don't have to stop to keep us up to date."

"No problem. Doing it now."

GPS on, and, within minutes, Shihab was back on the road. He felt that icy finger of fear down his spine again, and he didn't like it. He didn't like it at all. Where the hell was Said going?

Jo Jacobs and James, the other techie, were tracking Shihab through his GPS. They were also going through all the messages they had decoded. There were no places of departure, just what looked like random times, so Jo went back on the FfF website. Nothing. She pushed back from all the equipment, sat back in her chair, and closed her eyes. James looked on, wondering what she was doing, but not brave enough to ask. He continued tracking Shihab and noting down roads and street. Jo sat, perfectly still and silent, as she thought about all they had found, and where it had led them. Opening her eyes, she moved back towards the equipment, and began to search for the name of a booking agent. She had discovered that all travel arrangements for Nasir al Din Beshara had been booked by Saif Turay. Could he have also arranged Said's? Jo began her search.

James was tracking Shihab's movements: Adelaide Road, then Camden Street, when he realised where Said was heading. He was just a fraction behind Jo as she shouted, "Said's going to St Pancras. He's getting a train."

All hell broke loose.

James was sifting through the messages, trying to link trains and their destinations to the times they'd seen in the messages they'd decoded; Jo was phoning Adrian to update him. Adrian phoned the head of security at St Pancras, to get more men into the station. Maura was stuck at a red light behind a van, Jim had jumped out of the car and was trying to follow on foot, while Shihab, who had been so intent on not losing Said's car, had not seen the cyclist who pulled right in front of him, making him stand up on his brake and lose control of his bike. He slid along the road, trying to twist his bike away from the large articulated lorry towards which he was heading.

Meanwhile, Said had been dropped off at the station, had got on the train a couple of minutes before the time of departure, and was leaving St Pancras, carefully ensconced in a corner seat. He was totally unaware of the chaos that lay behind him, or of the presence of the heavily- built man who was trying to catch his breath after running to get on the train before it left. I'm getting too old for this, thought Jim.

Once he was in a seat with a view of Said, Jim texted Maura to tell her where he was. He wasn't sure where the train was going, but at least he was on it, and they hadn't lost Said. He was an old enough hand at this game to be able to innovate. Maura passed that message on to Alan Edwards who, in turn, passed it on to Adrian Smythe.

"Thank God for that," stated Adrian. "You really have an exceptional team. How's Shihab?"

"Nothing broken, just cuts and bruises and a strong desire to punch the cyclist in the face, which he restrained."

Although the situation was dire, Adrian took a moment to imagine how Shihab was feeling, and knew that the desire to maim was a reaction to nearly being killed. He knew that from experience.

"At least Jim's on the train, so we have eyes on Said still. Will get back to you once I've updated the PM. Don't think that will be an easy conversation."

"Rather you than me."

***

"What do you mean, Said's on a train? Does he have the ricin bomb with him?"

"We don't know but we don't think so."

"You don't think so?" the PM's voice rising in pitch.

Adrian's remained calm. "No, we don't think so. We believe the bomb will travel by other means, and he will get it when he gets to his final destination." "What's your next step?"

"We've got a very experienced operative on the train, so he's keeping us up to date. The technicians have worked out the times of the trains Said's catching, and from where, from the messages they've decoded. The thing we don't know is where he'll stay when he's too late to make his next connection from Rostock to Stockholm. I have arranged for operatives to be at the station so that they can follow him when he leaves. We will also have to change the operative on the train, so that his presence isn't obvious. We've arranged that too. The route Said's taking is unusual, in that he's going to Brussels, changing trains at Brussels-South railway to go to Rostock Stadthofen, then changing again to go to Stockholm."

"Why didn't he just fly, if he hasn't got the bomb with him?" "Not sure."

"But you are sure that that's how he's travelling, and that that's where he's going?"

"Yes."

"I'll update the Swedish Prime Minister. He's already said he will increase security on the day of his cabinet meeting, but he hasn't agreed to vaccinations. Stefan knows that he has to be careful not to give the game away, because, if the bomb does go off, the people will want to know why he couldn't stop it. But he still has to do the best he can to catch the bomber in the meantime. An unenviable situation to be in."

"Perhaps his security would have a good idea who might be involved in this. Or there may be some talk on the street about this sort of event. At least he would feel that he's doing something."

"Good point. If there's anything else I need you to do, I'll contact you."

Adrian leant back in his chair, and began picking at the cuff of his shirt, trying to break off a piece of loose cotton. The phone rang, and he was surprised to hear Ali's familiar voice. "Hi, Adrian. You obviously forgot to call me back, so I thought I'd call you."

"Sorry, Ali. Things have just been manic here. I did mean to call, but I really haven't had five minutes."

Ali could hear the tiredness in Adrian's voice.

"No worries. I had rung you to say that I'd been on the FfF website and it's obvious that Abdul-Azeem Tawfeek doesn't know that you've broken the code. I thought perhaps you could use that?"

"How do you know that that's the case?"

"I can't be absolutely certain, but the tone of his messages and content have much more information in them. There's also something that looks a little sinister about Muttaqi Saladin. Something about sleep talking. I thought at first it was sleep walking, but it isn't. Definitely sleep talking."

"That could explain a few things. Thanks, Ali."

"I haven't heard from Super Techie either. Any further developments?"

"I can't go into too much detail now but we do have a name, and we are tracking them as we speak. You've been a great help in all this and I appreciate it. Your finding out how dodgy the FfF website was gave us an entry into what was happening."

"Happy to help. I know you won't be able to tell me everything, but I would like to know how this all pans out in the end."

"Will do. Have to go now as I have some very important calls to make, but I will be in touch."

"Okay."

Ali put the phone down, and felt rather deflated. Adrian had said how helpful she'd been and everything, but now she felt flat and at a loose end. So much for spying. She decided to check the email account, and there was one in the draft box from Dan. She read it three times before she took in what it said. Then she was very angry indeed.

"I know I've only been away for a couple of weeks, but I thought there'd be a note saying how much you were missing me. Hope it's not out of sight, out of mind. Dan"

Chapter Twenty-One

Stefan Löfven paced up and down in front of the huge window in his office. The meeting with his cabinet had not gone well. Questions, questions and more questions! How could the British have allowed such a man to leave England? Why hadn't they stopped him? How did they know that there was a bomb, and that he was going to plant it in Rosenbad...? And so it had continued, until he had nearly lost his temper. In his calmest voice, he had reassured them that Theresa May didn't have to let them know what was happening. She wanted them all to work together to the same end: no bombs going off, no victims, no repercussions. Her team had been working non-stop to try to find out where the bomber was going, and it was only just before the individual had boarded a train that they had managed that. If they hadn't been so tenacious, the bomber would still be on his way, and they, the ruling party of this country, wouldn't have any idea of the chaos and bloodshed that was imminent for their people. That had silenced them - well, most of them. Stefan had also told them about the vaccine the British would provide as a preventative measure for the cabinet, if they wanted it. He had stressed that there would only be enough for the cabinet, as it was in short supply, and that there were some side effects. He advised them to think about what they wanted to do, and Cabinet would reconvene the next day, when he hoped to have more news.

***

Meanwhile, on the train, Jim watched as Said took a flask out of his backpack, the inside of which was a bright yellow colour, which surprised Jim, as Said didn't seem like a lover of yellow. Jim gave an ironic smile as he wondered how a lover of yellow should look. He froze when he saw Said unscrew the top of the flask, wondering whether Said did have the bomb, and whether he might be going to detonate it on the train. Jim was on the verge of dashing across the aisle and wrenching the flask out of Said's hands before he could open it, but he would have been too late to stop him. To his relief, Said poured a hot liquid out of the flask into the cup he held in his left hand. Jim could smell the strong, green tea from where he sat. He had managed to get a brief look in Said's backpack as he extracted the flask, and there seemed to be some clothes in the bag and little else. Good. Jim texted that information to Alan and got a reply back saying that he was to follow Said off the train and on to the platform, where someone else would take up his role following Said. He was to let Alan know when that had happened, and he would then be given further instructions. Jim was very tired, very hungry and glad that his part in the mission would soon be over. He wondered where Maura and Shihab were. He smiled again when he thought that Maura was clever enough to be okay, and Shihab was just Shihab

– invincible. He was pleased, forty-five minutes later, to hear the message on the train announcing its entry into Brussels. He watched as Said took some tickets out of his wallet, and seemed to be checking them. Jim noticed that there was quite a pile of them, so, obviously, Said was travelling on somewhere. Jim hoped that Alan knew where that was, and that the people who would take over from him were up to scratch. He felt sure that they would be.

Said picked up his backpack, and slipped his arms into the straps. He didn't look very happy: a frown crossing his forehead, downturned lips, with a thin layer of moisture just above the top lip. His anxiety was almost palpable. Jim wondered whether he had volunteered to plant the bomb, or whether he had been coerced into it. It wouldn't be the first time that that had happened. Said moved closer to the exit doors, and Jim was just a couple of people behind him. The train lurched into the station; the woman in front of Said opened the door and got out of the carriage, followed by Said and the few people behind him. Jim scanned the people on the platform, and was pleased to see a familiar face. He walked past Said, and went to stand by a pillar on the platform, watching while his replacement (Jake Randall) moved to a place where Said could be watched without its being too obvious. Said was approached by a youngish couple, who leaned in to him as they spoke. Said was no actor; he looked relieved. This couple must be there to meet him, thought Jim. Said followed behind them, as they led him to a restaurant just outside the station. Jake duly followed behind them, while Jim was waiting for instructions on how he was to proceed now he had been replaced. Work as a team with Jake, and, once Said's next train (the 1.11 a.m. to Rostock) had departed with Said and Jake on board, straight back home, was his directive. Fine by me, thought Jim, as he knew that he would be able to get a few hours' sleep on the train, which he knew he would be in dire need of by then. Jake was an experienced agent, who had the ability to merge into any surroundings. Jim was happy to relinquish the surveillance of Said to him. Jim ambled slowly out of the station, and took up post at a café, from which he had a clear view of the restaurant which Said had entered. He ordered a light dish, so that he wouldn't have to wait too long, in case Said and his friends decided to leave the restaurant quicker than he hoped. Jake was well-hidden in a cul-de-sac opposite the restaurant.

After a couple of hours, Said and his new friends left the restaurant, and headed back to the station. Jim had already paid his bill, and was having his second coffee, so he was able to leave his seat with relative ease, and without appearing to be in a rush. Said went into the waiting room, while his friends went to check the platform from which his train would leave. They returned about ten minutes later, and sat on either side of Said. Quiet and calm conversations seemed to be the order of the day, and Said was looking more relaxed. As Jake was in a position to see Said, Jim had followed the friends to the board, which had departure times and platforms, in the hope that he might be able to overhear some of their conversation.

"He doesn't look very special to me," muttered the woman, "in fact, he's quite boring."

"We were told that he was a special guest, and that we had to look after him, feed him and make sure he gets on the 1.11 a.m. train to Rostock Stadthofen. We don't need," he hesitated, "or want to know why he's special."

"But why Rostock?" she continued.

The man with her grabbed her arm so quickly, she had only time to let out a low moan, as he squeezed it with some venom.

"Shut up asking questions! We were told to do it, and we have no option. Your questions will put us in harm's way." He gave another squeeze and then let go of her arm.

The woman was tempted to continue, but stopped when she saw the almost maniacal look on the man's face. She knew when she had overstepped the mark, and this was one of those times.

"I'm sorry," she whispered. "I won't ask again."

The man merely glanced at her, with contempt in his eyes.

"Come, back to our guest. We know the platform and will make sure he gets on the right train. Then we're done."

The woman meekly followed behind him, not daring to rub her arm, which throbbed with pain.

Said was pleased to see them back. He was feeling very anxious, and needed to have someone to talk to, so that he didn't focus on what he had to do when he got to his final destination. They talked about the weather, the food in the restaurant, everything and nothing. Everything that was nothing to him. At 12.30 a.m., the man got out of his seat and walked around the waiting room. He whispered to Said that it was time to go to the platform for his next train. Said eased himself stiffly out of the seat. He was not used to sitting for long periods of time, and he knew that his next journey was for almost twelve hours. He hoped that he would be able to get some sleep, as he was beginning to feel exhausted. He was shepherded along various platforms and stairs, until he arrived at the correct platform. Said and the couple sat together on a bench on the platform and waited. No more conversations. The train pulled into the station, and only five people disembarked. Said got on the train, gave a weak wave goodbye to the couple, found his seat, and settled down for a long journey. Jim watched all this, while Jake got on the train and found a seat from which he could observe Said. Ten minutes later, the train was leaving the station, chugging along on its journey to Rostock Stadthofen, totally unaware of the person it was carrying. Jim made his way to the platform for his train back to St Pancras, and was glad when it arrived, and he was on his journey home. Another couple were walking out of the station, keeping Said's friends in sight. They would follow them, and find out where they lived. It was probable that they would have to be picked up for questioning in the very near future.

***

In Stockholm, the security services were frantically searching through their files to identify anyone who might be connected to what was going on. They had been given the information about the FfF website, and were looking for anyone they knew who could be involved. Having the key to the code on that website, supplied by Jo Jacobs, aka Super Techie, they were able to sift quickly through messages. One or two names were appearing with some frequency, although the messages seemed quite innocuous. A key name was Abdul-Alee Khatib who was a regular visitor to Sweden. Checks would be made to see whether he was on any flights coming into Sweden. The team would persevere throughout the night, and would, in fact, come up with a couple of names that might be useful. Operatives would be put on those names, to see with whom they were associating, and where they could be found. Several addresses had been found for Khatib, and they all were under observation. Resources were already being stretched, but that couldn't be helped. Time was of the essence, and they were all aware of that.

The next morning, Stefan Löfven met again with his cabinet. Although the atmosphere was dour, his cabinet seemed more responsive to the situation, and what had been done up until then. They had all decided that they would not have the vaccine, as they wanted to show their faith in the security services of their country and the UK. They knew that they were taking a grave chance, but they believed that they were doing the right thing. A more selfish reason, for some, was that, if the bomb went off, people were killed, and it became known that the cabinet had had pre-knowledge of the ricin bomb, and so had been vaccinated, the politicians would feel the wrath of the people. They would not understand the scarcity of the vaccine, and the need to ensure that a stable government continued if such a catastrophe occurred. There was some discussion about calling off the celebrations, but the vote was in favour of continuing as normal. Stefan commented that cancelling the celebrations would in fact be a retrograde step, as it could mean that the bomber would panic, and would set the bomb off prematurely. At least now they knew the target and the planned time of attack, which they hoped would help them to catch the bomber before he set the bomb off. Stefan closed the cabinet meeting with one final comment.

"I know that you are worried for your families, but you must not – and I stress not – tell your family about what is going on, or send them away out of Stockholm. That would raise suspicions, and we can't afford for any information to leak to the press or anyone else. We are all in the same boat. We have to trust the security services to do the job for which they are so well-trained. That's all we can do at this time. And, if you are a believer, pray."

The cabinet members, eyes downcast, left the chamber. Stefan stood tall until they had all left, then slumped back into his chair. He believed what he'd said about the security services, and he hoped he wasn't wrong.

Chapter Twenty-Two

Abdul-Alee Khatib arrived at Stockholm airport at one of the busiest times of day. Visitors were travelling to see the sights, and timing their visit for the mini-celebrations; businessmen were returning from meetings, eyes glued to their phones, as if their lives depended upon it; people had come to work on stalls and in booths at the celebrations, and school children had arrived on visits. So many. So unlucky. He smiled: not something he often did, but his thoughts were a few days in the future, when he could visualise the inert corpses of the same visitors, all worthy, he believed, of their fate. As his private plane regularly flew into Stockholm, he knew that the security services wouldn't take much notice of him and his meagre luggage when they were so busy. He knew that he would be fast-tracked. However, not one for taking chances, he had given a small suitcase (one with the backpack and bombs in) to a friend, who had flown with him, telling him that it contained fragile items. If they were stopped, Khatib would deny all knowledge of the suitcase. He would only be in Stockholm for thirty-six hours; that was enough time to leave the bombs for Said, and return to the safety of England.

As he knew that he would be, Khatib was fast-tracked, and was soon on his way to the house of one of his friends, feeling very pleased with himself. He wouldn't have been quite so arrogant if he'd realised that he was only fast-tracked because his name had been red-flagged for security reasons. The instruction that had been given was to let him through as soon as the security operatives were in position to watch him, and follow him wherever he went. As he sauntered out of the airport, Khatib was thinking about Abdul-Azeem Tawfeek. He had done well to find Mustafa Younan, a young man with amazing skills, who would be useful to them for a long time. Finding Said Ishak, too, had been done well; a lamb to the slaughter. Khatib reflected on how the mission could have failed badly if they had sent Said on a plane. It was a good job that Nasir al Din Beshara had discovered how obviously anxious Said was in an airport. It was only by the Prophet's help that the new route by train had been decided upon. Having a man who didn't ask questions about booking a journey, as long as a good fee was paid, was an added bonus. Life was good.

The car took him the relatively short distance to the house in which he was staying. He was greeted warmly at the door by an elderly man, and quickly moved into the house. The team following Khatib texted that information to the key man in their control centre, once they were in a position to keep sight of the front door. Anders, in the control centre, added that information to the whiteboard on which they had names, addresses and any other information which they hoped would be useful in identifying where the bomb would be placed and when. Would knowing that there were two bombs to be placed have led him to do anything differently? Probably not. The team would follow Khatib if he left the property, and would take note of anyone who entered or left the house, taking pictures as and when they could. With the improvement in technology, a phone was able to do all that had previously needed numerous pieces of equipment. It was the technology which had helped the security services to get this far in such a short space of time, and it was hoped that it would be the means to stop the bomber.

While events were moving along swiftly in Stockholm, the train in which Said was travelling was doing the same. Slumped in his seat, Said's eyes were closed, but he was unable to sleep. He was reliving the story of the Prophet meeting Michael the Archangel for the first time, recognising in Him the same fears that he, Said, felt at this moment. He was heartened, because he knew that the Prophet conquered His fears, and went on to do great things, and he hoped that he'd be able to do the same. Said recited the words of the Koran under his breath. He wasn't a scholar, but had learned the prayers by rote, just like the Prophet. He felt himself to be stronger and more in control when he prayed those beautiful words. Said drifted off into a dreamless sleep, a smile on his face, and his mission clear in his mind.

Jake, watching Said, wasn't able to sleep. He felt his eyes begin to droop, and knew he must fight his tiredness. Standing by his seat, he tensed his leg muscles, then stretched them gently, before walking slowly up the aisle to the toilet area. He washed his hands, splashed water on his face, and then began the journey back to his seat, giving

Said a cursory glance as he passed. His expression turned to stone when he saw the smile on Said's face, wondering whether the thought of killing lots of people gave him that much pleasure. He had to control himself as he struggled with an intense desire to grab Said and pound his face to a pulp to wash the smile away. Breathe, breathe, he was thinking, but his body was taking time to adjust to a calmer state. Professional that he was, the turmoil that was Jake was not evident to anyone else at that moment. He hadn't realised how tense he had been until he sat back in his seat and felt the tension shift. He was now aware of a grade one, screaming headache. Damn it. Three tablets and two bottles of water later, the headache diminished if he kept his head still and his eyes closed. He was able to do this for ten minutes, before he fell asleep, his head resting on a window whose cold surface helped alleviate the pain in his head.

An hour later, the train shuddered as it careered around a tight corner; Jake's head was thrown off the window, and he woke with a start. It took him a few seconds to be fully awake, and, when he looked over to the seat where Said had been sitting, he was gone. Panic! What to do next? He was just getting up when he saw Said making his way back to his seat from the direction of the toilet. Jake eased back into his seat in time to hear the message saying that they would be arriving at Rostock Stadthofen in fifty-five minutes. There was an apology, because they would be twenty-five minutes later than scheduled. He felt the vibration of an incoming text on his phone. His instruction was very similar to Jim's.

Stay with Said until the new operative was in place, then get a train back. He was not to follow Said, and whoever turned up to meet him, because Said would be staying somewhere, so that he could catch the 1.37 p.m. train to Stockholm the next day.

Two women met Said off the train: one elderly, one much younger. They embraced him as if he was a relative, but Said's stiff return gave a lie to that. He allowed himself to be escorted out of the terminal to a waiting VW van, in which a very old man sat in the driving seat. Said got in the front, and the two women got in the back. The new operative (Mike James) followed Said out of the station, mounted an old motorbike, and began the pursuit. Behind him, on another motorbike, was the second member of the new team, Jayne Neat.

After an uneventful twenty-minute journey, the van pulled up outside a block of flats. Said and the women got out, and the van drove off. Mike parked his bike and followed the trio into the entrance of the flats. He was just in time to see the lift disappearing. It stopped on the seventh floor. This was a problem, as there were four flats on each floor and it could be any one of them. Mike was replaced by Jayne, while he went outside and phoned Anders in the command centre. He told him where he was, and what had happened. Anders said that they had received a couple of photos from Jake Randall, that Jake had taken of the women who had met Said off the train. They were running them through facial recognition software, to see whether they could find any matches. They hadn't been successful so far. Mike said that they'd stay close by the entrance to the flats until they had further instructions, in case Said or any of the women came out. Anders agreed that that was the best option at that time.

**

In Stockholm, Abdul-Alee Khatib was in a small room at the back of the house, checking the equipment which had been gathered for Said Ishak. He was pleased to see that it was all there, including some very bright yellow clothes. Khatib took the black backpack out of the suitcase, and placed it carefully towards the back of a table near the door, so that it couldn't fall. He wasn't sure that a fall would make the bombs go off, but he wasn't prepared to take that risk. "You have done well, my friend," Khatib stated, a smile almost splitting his round face. "When the special guest comes, the day after tomorrow, you are to allow him to shower first, eat and then bring him into this room. He must then be left to pray and prepare. What he has to do will be done the next day."

The elderly man merely nodded his head in obedience, while Khatib glanced around the room. He could almost taste his success, knowing that, when the bombs went off, and so many died, he would have been the conduit that had made it happen. Praise be to the Prophet.

"We will eat in an hour, then we will pray. In three hours, my car will be here, and I will return to the airport, to catch my flight at nine p.m."

"As the Prophet wills," replied the old man. "As the Prophet wills, indeed."

Chapter Twenty-Three

Anders, in the control centre, jumped when he heard a ping from the computer. Could it be a result, in such a short time? The picture of the older woman who had met Said had been identified as Nessa Wakim, a known anti-government agitator. She hadn't been seen around for quite a while, so Anders wondered whether she'd been keeping a low profile so that she could be involved in the proposed bombing. She was a nasty piece of work, who was known to have hurt a few of the younger Muslim girls in her area, because she had said that they were being traitors to the one true religion. She disapproved of the modern clothes they wore, and of the fact that they had friends who were not Muslim. It was only because her family had such high status that she had got away with such behaviour, as the young girls were afraid to speak against her. He could now contact the team to tell them that she lived in Flat 7C. The people in flat 7A and 7B were not known to the authorities, and flat 7D was currently empty. Anders sent Marta, his second-in-command, to collect the keys to 7D from the office where they were kept. The manager was not happy about the demand for the keys, but he wasn't given a choice. Marta was not someone whom you would want to annoy or upset. Within minutes, the two team members were in 7D, keeping watch through the peephole in the door. They also had thermal imaging goggles, so that they could 'see' how many people were in 7C. It would, they knew, be a long evening for them.

In London, Adrian Smythe was bringing the PM up to date with events and it wasn't going well.

"Have you found out where the bomb is yet?"

"I'm afraid not but…"

"There can be no buts. If that bomb is set off, it would be a catastrophe, with dire consequences."

"I do know that and we are following up a very good lead…"

"How good?"

"We won't know until we've finished following it up." Adrian was getting angry, and trying his best not to let it sound in his voice. He was glad he wasn't doing face to face, as he wasn't sure he'd have been able to hide his feelings. Get a grip, he thought.

"What's the time frame?"

"With respect, I can't tell you what I don't know. What I can tell you is that the bomber is being tracked and observed, and we know the times of his trains and his arrival times; a man we believe may have taken the bomb into Stockholm has arrived at that destination and has a flight booked back to England for 9 p.m. this evening. That's as much as we know at the moment, but things are changing even as we speak."

Silence.

"Was there anything else you wanted to know?" Adrian, breaking the uneasy silence, finally asked.

"There are lots of questions I'd like answered, but now isn't the time. Keep me in the loop." Adrian sat back in his chair, ran his hands through his hair and sighed. It would all work out. It had to.

While having a quick bite to eat and a coffee, Adrian updated the white board with the new information he'd received. They were close, he knew that, and he hoped there wouldn't be any problems at the last minute. Until they knew where Said Ishak was going in Stockholm, there was little else they could do. Adrian was liaising with Anders in Stockholm, so they were both kept up to speed with what was happening, where it was happening and when. There was a team following and observing Said, while another team was following and observing people who could be involved. Adrian knew that Abdul-Alee Khatib was a key player in what was happening. He also knew that Khatib's leaving Stockholm after such a short visit was a good indicator that he had carried the bomb, and was leaving before it was placed and detonated. Definitely one to keep an eye on. It suddenly occurred to Adrian that they could get a closer look at what Khatib was doing.

"Hi, Ali, I wondered if you could do me a favour?"

Ali, surprised to hear from Adrian, was only too happy to have something else to do, as she'd been feeling like a spare part.

"I'm sure I can. What would you like me to do?"

"We believe we're getting close to the bomb being planted, and we know that Abdul-Alee Khatib is a key player. Can you stay on the FfF website and monitor what, if any, messages he is sending, decoding them as they're put on the website? We have the key to the code, but he doesn't know that. He may give something away that will help us."

"That's not a problem. I'd be glad to help. What do you want me to do if I get anything?"

"The best thing would be to pass anything on to Super Techie. He can link it to what he's already got, and feed back to me if and when we have any links."

"Great. Will get on it now. You were lucky to catch me, as I've been out at my tai chi class this morning and only just got in."

"Thanks, Ali. You've been a great help in all this."

As he put down the phone, Adrian got that flush of pleasure again. He liked Ali and was attracted to her no-nonsense attitude to things, and her desire to help others. Dan was a lucky man, but Adrian was sure Dan knew that.

In Stockholm, Anders had updated his prime minister on what was happening and where. Stefan Löfven had listened intently, made some comments, and then directed Anders to keep him up to date with what was happening. Just one more journey before the bomber is in my city, Stefan was thinking. He sighed and then shook himself, not allowing himself to sink into apathy. The bomber was being observed and followed, houses were being kept under observation, and some known people had been identified. Stefan knew that they had done as much as they could at this point. He realised that the next forty-eight hours were crucial, and that he would be no use to anyone if he hadn't slept. Closing the file on his desk, Stefan looked around his office, put the file in a drawer, locked it, and then pushed his chair back from the desk. He would go home, and he would sleep. Tomorrow he would be fresh, and ready to deal with whatever was to come. With heavy feet and a heavier heart, Stefan left his office and made his way down to his car. He would be home within half an hour, and in bed not long after that. Sleep would come, and he hoped that sleep was dreamless. His worry was that the dreams would be full of death and pain and failure. Stefan reminded himself that dreams were not reality, but were a possibility, or a fear. He wouldn't let himself be overcome by fear; he couldn't afford to be that self-indulgent.

Said tossed and turned in the small bed in the flat, unable to sleep. Although he wasn't tall, he was rather broad, and the single bed was too narrow and had a lumpy mattress. Said knew that he shouldn't be annoyed that he was uncomfortable, but he knew if he was to be successful in doing what the Prophet wanted, he had to get a good night's sleep. He was on the verge of sleep when he heard raised voices in the next room. Although he couldn't hear what they were saying, he could tell by the tone that it was an argument. Said strained to hear what they were saying, but was unsuccessful. He had just put his feet out of the bed when he heard a loud slap, following by the sound of a woman crying. Then, the harsh voice of the older woman who had met him from the station.

"You'll do what you're told and wear what you're told. You are nothing. You came from nothing. You own nothing. Your life belongs to me. Do you understand?"

Silence.

Another loud slap, but, this time, no tears.

"Do you understand?"

Said couldn't hear what was said, but the crying stopped, and no more voices were heard.

Getting back into bed, Said lay down but was awake for quite a long time, trying to understand what he'd heard. In the end, he got out of bed, knelt on the floor and began to recite the prayers that he so loved from the Koran. The Prophet would protect and guide him.

In 7D, Mike and Jayne could hear the argument. They didn't intervene, because they knew that Said had gone to bed, and that it was the two women who were arguing. They waited, ready to break into Flat 7C if they had to, but hoping that that wasn't the case, because, if they broke cover, they wouldn't know where Said had intended to go in Stockholm to plant his bomb, and there could be a back-up bomber about whom they didn't know. Both of them were relieved when the argument stopped, and the flat fell silent.

Chapter Twenty-Four

Abdul-Alee Khatib was not happy at all. He had been at the airport for quite a while, and was still waiting to go through to the airport lounge.

"Why am I still here, and not in the airport lounge, waiting to board my plane, which takes off at nine p.m.?"

"I'm very sorry, Sir," replied the woman seated at the check-in desk. "I'm afraid we have problems with the belt which takes luggage down to the lower room from where it's put on the carts and taken to the planes."

Without giving her time to continue, Khatib answered sharply, "But I don't have any luggage, so surely I could be checked in?"

"I'm afraid not, Sir, as there may not be any planes taking off at all if we can't get the luggage on. That means we may have to change flight plans to accommodate the delay, so your plane may not be able to take off at nine p.m."

"Do you have any idea at all how long it will take to sort out the fault?"

"Not at this time."

Khatib turned away in disgust. He was so angry that he wanted to pull the woman over the counter and punch her in the face. He had to get out of Stockholm as soon as possible, and was considering other options he had.

Anders, in the control room in Stockholm, was

receiving a live feed of the interaction between Khatib and the woman at the check-in desk. He could see in Khatib's face how angry he was, and how difficult it was for him, trying not to show it. Khatib's reaction reinforced their thinking: the bomb was in Stockholm and the detonation was soon, hence Khatib's desire to leave Stockholm as quickly as possible.

Two hours later, check-in desks were opened, and passengers were processed and sent to the various gates for their flights. Khatib's plane had been given the 2 a.m. slot the next day. He was still very angry, but looked relieved as he went through security. While he'd been waiting in the airport, Khatib had been putting messages on the FfF website via his phone, updating his colleagues on what had been happening. He would have been beyond angry if he'd realised that all his messages, and their replies, were being decoded with indecent haste, and their content passed on to the security services.

***

"Yes, he's saying the package is in place and the owner is arriving early the next day. The message was sent at one a.m.," Ali replied to Super Techie's enquiry.

"That ties in with what we know about the time Ishak's train arrives in Stockholm. That's so helpful, Ali. It helps confirm we're on the right path. Keep on the site, and hope to speak with you soon."

Ali ended the call, feeling happy that she'd been able to help Super Techie and Adrian in this matter. She only hoped that they could stop the bomber now, before he had time to plant his bomb. A cup of Jasmine tea was next for her, to keep her bright and alert while she continued to monitor the FfF website. All in a day's work for a spy!

***

Said Ishak was feeling rather uncomfortable. He hadn't enjoyed his stay in the flat. He hadn't liked the old woman, whose mean and spiteful looks made him feel very uncomfortable. He really wasn't happy that the old woman and her daughter were now travelling with him on the last leg of his journey. How could he find the peace he needed, with her cold eyes watching him? How could he find his inner peace when her daughter, sitting at his side, had the saddest eyes he'd ever seen? Nessa, the old woman, had told him that, travelling together, they looked like a normal Muslim family so others would not be curious about them. She knew where they had to go when they arrived in Stockholm and who would be meeting them. Said had no choice but to do what she told him.

Anders had been told that Nessa, and her daughter, Meena, would be accompanying Ishak on the train, and had alerted the operatives at Stockholm to be extra-cautious. Nessa was an old hand at identifying when she was being observed or followed, and could, and would, take evasive and decisive action if she thought that they were under threat. Although they had been unable to charge her with anything, they knew that she had been a key player in a few abductions and murders, but knowing and proving were two very different things.

The train rattled into the station at Stockholm at 6.30

a.m. exactly. The 'family' collected their luggage: Said his black backpack, and Meena a small, overnight bag. The operative on the train observing them kept in his seat. The new team was waiting on the platform, and would pick up surveillance when the 'family' left the train. As everyone else disembarked, Jake Randall got up slowly and left the train. He headed to a café at the end of the platform, ordered a coffee, sat down and waited for further instructions. He would be staying in Stockholm until the bomber was caught.

An old green VW van pulled up outside the station. Nessa got in the front, and Meena and Said got in the back. Traffic was just building up, but was still reasonably light, so the woman on the motorbike behind them had to be careful that she wasn't spotted. The car following behind her kept to a steady speed, ready to overtake her, should the need arise. The journey was comparatively short. As the van stopped outside a small house, the door was opened, and an elderly man greeted them warmly and ushered them inside. The woman on the motorbike gave a mere nod of her head to the member of the surveillance team who she knew was watching the house. How arrogant of Khatib to be so comfortable with his plan, even though he had so recently visited the same house! The photograph taken by Jake on the train as the 'family' had collected their luggage, had shown Said to have a small black package. Khatib's friend, when they visited together, had carried a small suitcase. Could it have held a similar backpack to Said's? Could the bomb be in that, if it did? It wouldn't be long before they found out.

147

Chapter Twenty-Five

The two men, Abdul-Azeem Tawfeek and Abdul-Alee Khatib, greeted each other warmly at the entrance to the Zakaria Masjd Mosque. Their smiles were a reflection of the joy they felt that the plan they had hatched, to bring pain and terror to the unbelievers, was so close to fruition. Entering the mosque, they went into the back room, knelt down and began to pray together. Their hearts were so full of hatred that they could no longer feel the beauty of the prayers from the Koran, or the joy from saying the precious words of the Prophet. They recited them as if they were children regurgitating times tables or verbs from other languages, things that had little meaning or understanding.

Meanwhile, frantic action was taking place. Adrian had been involved in a video conference with Theresa May and Stefan Löfven, bringing both up to date. Also included in the call had been Anders, from the control centre in Stockholm, who had even more recent information concerning the whereabouts of Said Ishak and the connection to Khatib.

"Yes, it is the same house Khatib visited and was so keen to leave," Anders stated.

"How many operatives do you have on this now?" asked Adrian.

"We have two teams, five in each team,

interchangeable as and when needed, so it isn't obvious what they're about."

"Sounds good. What else can we do from this end?"

"You're already monitoring the FfF website, the Zakaria Masjd Mosque is under observation, as are some of the main players, and your technician is keeping us up to speed with anything new that you find. At the moment, that's all we can ask."

"Okay. You've also received the vaccine?"

"Yes, it's stored in a safe place, and, hopefully, we won't need it."

"Is there anything more we can do for you, Stefan?" asked Theresa.

"Not at the moment. We're now formulating our plan to pick up the bomber before he sets off his bomb. We know it must be soon, as the celebrations are tomorrow," he replied. "Our most experienced technician has written a program which can activate the webcam on computers. They must have a computer in the house if they've been sending and receiving messages through the FfF website. She may already have got the camera working there. I'll check with her, and get back to you as soon as possible," stated Adrian.

At this point the video conference closed.

"Jo, you're still monitoring the program to activate the webcam on the computers of people sending messages through the FfF website?" asked Adrian.

"Yes, why?" replied Jo Jacobs.

"I'm sending you a name and address in Stockholm. There must have been messages sent from and to this address via the FfF website. I need to know what's happening in that house as soon as possible."

"I'm on it. Get back to you as soon as I can."

"Has to be sooner than that!"

"Okay, I get it."

Jo went hot, then cold, then hot again. The elderly man sitting at the keyboard was typing very slowly into the message box on the FfF website. Jo was decoding the message as he typed. *Package received. Equipment here. Package will be set mid-morning.*

Adrian picked up on the first ring. Jo filled him in on what she'd found and he, in turn, relayed that information to the two prime ministers and Anders. All Adrian could do now was wait.

Stefan made the decision that the operatives who would enter the house would be vaccinated. There was to be no choice. They could sort out any side effects afterwards; hopefully there'd be an "afterwards". They still didn't know how secure the ricin was, how the bomb to deliver the ricin was set up, and where the bomb was. They just knew (or hoped they knew) the bomb was in the house. It was decided that they would enter the house at 4 a.m., silently and swiftly. If people had been up all night, that was the time when they would have started to struggle to keep awake, and might even have dropped off to sleep. If they were lucky. They had to hope that no one was up praying.

Anders gave the instructions to the members of the teams, in a calm and confident voice. Now was not the time to overthink what they had to do. Sweeping through the house, they were to look for anything which could hold a bomb. If found, they were to leave it where they found it, secure the room and let the others know: a simple plan. All the operatives were armed, and all the guns had silencers fitted. No one was to be shot unless there was no other alternative. The team members understood that instruction very well. If they couldn't find the bomb, they were to gather all the people in the house into one room and hold them there until more help arrived.

At 3.45 a.m., all the operatives were in place and ready to move in when given the signal. Those fifteen minutes up to 4 p.m. seemed to pass so slowly. Finally, it was time. The house was not very secure, with simple locks in place, and no alarm system. The locks were soon opened with lock picks. Members of the team moved slowly through the bottom of the house, listening at doors before quietly opening them. The team who entered through the front door searched the lounge first, then moved into the dining room. The furniture in both rooms was old but well-polished, but nothing of significance was found, so they moved towards the kitchen. The team who entered through the back door came into the kitchen. They found the usual things you find in a kitchen: cooker, table and chairs, etc., but nothing out of place. However, when they moved into a room off the kitchen they were surprised to find a racing bike. It was brightly coloured and new. At the side of it were some lycra shorts, a top in bright yellow and a black hat. A small black backpack was on the table. It was bright yellow inside but all it had in it were two Nalgene water bottles. Members of the team looked around, and couldn't find anything else. As they went to walk out of the room, one of them was looking bemused.

"What's wrong?" asked one of the others.

"Why would you have two water bottles? There's only space for one on the bike"

"Well, I suppose…"

Taking one of the bottles out of the bag, the woman who had followed the 'family' from the station on a motorbike put her face very close to the bottle.

"Shit! The bomb's in the bottle."

"But there are two bottles, so are there two bombs?" her team mate asked.

Even more carefully, she took out the other bottle, put her face close to it, and pulled it back quickly. She put both bottles gingerly on the table and backed away.

"Yep!"

They edged out of the room, and closed the door very quietly.

The woman stood guard on the door, while her partner went to find the others. He met them entering the kitchen. He explained very quickly what they'd found, that his partner had secured the room, and that he was going outside to call Anders. He told the others to go upstairs and secure the rest of the house, moving the occupants from their rooms into the sitting room. He reminded them to take care, as they didn't know what, if any, weapons the occupants might have.

Said was woken by the screaming. He thought he'd been having a nightmare, but came awake fully when he felt hands dragging him out of bed. The screams were from Nessa, who had reacted violently when she was awoken by strange hands. She had cut the arm of one of the men and was struggling forward, trying to cut the throat of one of the others. Although not a young woman, she had the strength of the possessed and it took two of the men to disarm and restrain her. That didn't stop her shrieking and shouting and trying to kick out. Nessa cursed them all, while her daughter stood, fear etched over her young face, wondering what would happen to them now.

As if in a dream, Said struggled to make sense of what was happening. Shaking his head to clear his thoughts, the realisation came that he had failed the Prophet. He would not be able to complete his mission. Said began to cry tears of remorse, rocking backwards and forwards in the chair.

"Holy Prophet help me!" he wailed. "I want only to do Your will!"

The team members looked on in disbelief. Didn't Said realise that he would have killed thousands? Why would he want to do that?

His wails grew louder and louder, and he began to rock faster and faster. Suddenly, he jumped up and made a dash for the door of the sitting room. He got to the handle of the door when large, strong hands picked him up and almost threw him back into the chair. "Stay there!"

Said jumped up, screaming and thrashing about. Once again, he was thrown back in the chair.

Said turned and looked at Nessa, feeling her eyes cutting into him, judgemental and spiteful. "You are the curse that has stopped me doing the Prophet's will. On my own, I would have succeeded," Said sobbed.

"You are nothing. You have failed the Prophet because you are nothing," Nessa sneered.

Said dived at her and managed to catch her round the neck. She, however, was stronger and nastier than Said could ever be. She grabbed a heavy bookend from the sideboard and banged him on the side of the head with it. Said fell to the floor, blood gushing from his wound, and lay still. Nessa then tried to use the same weapon to hit one of the team who was bending down to attend to Said. Luckily, he managed to move his head out of the way and she hit him on his shoulder. It took two men to take the improvised weapon from her and get her back in her seat. The sooner she was under lock and key the better. The elderly man who owned the house and Meena sat silently, watching all that went on, and worrying about what would happen to them.

Chapter Twenty-Six

Stefan had to decide what to do next. It would make sense to evacuate all those who lived close to the house before they went in, to move the bombs, in case they went off. Two bombs, not one: that was a shock! However, Stefan knew that, if the bombs went off, the people in those houses would die anyway, so would it make sense to leave them be and move the bombs quietly? In the end, he decided to evacuate them, so that the men in the NBC suits could go into the premises and remove the bombs, taking them to a secure location where they could be defused without distributing the ricin they contained. In the end, it didn't take very long to remove them. The house was then sealed.

Nessa Wakim would tell them nothing when she was interviewed. All she did throughout the interview was rant and scream, and try to attack anyone who came within grabbing distance. Her daughter, Meena, was different. Shy and timid, she responded positively to her interrogators who had so far treated her kindly, despite the situation she was in. Meena explained that her mother had told her she was going to die for the Prophet. When she had said that she didn't want to die, Nessa had denigrated her and slapped her. She had been made to go on the train. She liked Said, and felt they were similar personalities, but had been scared to talk with him in case of reprisal from her mother. Said was to dress in the cycling clothes, putting one of the bombs in the bottle on his bike and the other in his backpack, bright yellow side out. He would cycle near Rosenbad, and leave the bottle from his bag on the floor near a small garden, as if he'd been sitting down and forgotten it. He would then cycle a bit further on and go into the toilets with his backpack, leaving the bike outside. Inside the toilets he would change into ordinary clothes from his backpack, turn it so the black side was showing, not the yellow, put his clothes in the bin and walk out. Nessa was to be waiting close by, and they would walk off together. The bombs would go off half an hour later. Her interrogators asked her if she knew what was in the bombs. Meena looked confused and shook her head, replying that they were just bombs.

Said was in hospital, and still unconscious. It wasn't known whether he would survive. Scans had shown a blood clot in his brain, from the angry blow he had received from Nessa. Surgeons felt that it was unwise to operate at that time. There were two men from the security team keeping watch night and day, in case Said came around. There were two other casualties. One of the men in the security team had gone into spasm shortly after being vaccinated against ricin. He'd been rushed into hospital in a coma. He was in isolation, and was being cared for by a doctor who had previously worked on the ricin vaccine. The other casualty was female. She had developed a rash and a high temperature, had then begun to have difficulty breathing, and had collapsed minutes before the team entered the house in which Said was staying. She had died on her way to hospital. A third casualty of all this, perhaps, was Muttaqi Saladin, whose whereabouts were still unknown.

In England, Adrian had just finished a call with the PM. He was so relieved that the bombs had been found before they could be detonated. Teams had been sent to arrest Abdul-Alee Khatib and Abdul-Azeem Tawfeek, and they were in custody waiting to be interviewed. Adrian believed that the evidence they had on the two men would be enough to put them away for a long time. He was still worried about the radicalisation of young men in the Zaria Masjd Mosque, wondering if that would continue if the two men currently in custody were given prison sentences. They hadn't been able to get anything conclusive on Nasir al Din Beshara, but were hopeful that the interview they were having with Said Turay, who did all his travel arrangements, might be helpful.

A major worry for Adrian was: who had made the ricin bombs? That was something they were still trying to pursue. He also was aware that the quantities of castor beans that had been bought could make a lot of ricin, much more than was in the two bombs. The war's not won yet, he thought, but we have won this battle.

"Yes, it is good news, and your department was a major player in that. So well done!"

"Thanks, Adrian; it is my job. I've some other good news for you as well."

"My cup runneth over," Adrian joked.

"It may just do that! The program Ali sent me that

I've been trying to adapt to trace who's on the Dark Web is showing some very promising results. Now I've got time to work on it, I may be able to perfect it to do the job."

"Wow! That is good news. Double well done."

"My pleasure."

***

Ali was very excited. Dan was arriving home from his trip that evening, and she was looking forward to seeing him. She'd been swimming that morning, had had a great afternoon out with her friend Geraldine and was preparing Dan's favourite meal: a huge mixed grill! At seven thirty p.m., Dan arrived home, feeling tired but happy to be back. Pushing open the door, he could see Ali sitting on the sofa, smiling, a glass of Sauvignon Blanc in her hand. She got up, kissed and hugged him.

"Just one thing I want to ask you before you take your suitcases upstairs?"

"Okay," replied Dan, thinking Ali was going to tell him how much she'd missed him, or ask what present he'd got her.

"Tell me about your relationship with Adrian Smythe."

Dan opened his mouth to speak, then closed it again when he saw the determined set of Ali's jaw. "Bugger!"